DODGE: FINDING HIS JEWEL

PJ FIALA

ROLLING THUNDER PUBLISHING

COPYRIGHT

Printed in the United States of America

First published 2019

Fiala, PJ

Dodge: Finding His Jewel / PJ Fiala

p. cm.

1. Romance—Fiction. 2. Romance—Suspense. 3. Romance - Military

I. Title – Dodge: Finding His Jewel

Paperback ISBN: 978-1942618508

DEDICATION

I've had so many wonderful people come into my life and I want you all to know how much I appreciate it. From each and every reader who takes the time out of their days to read my stories and leave reviews, thank you.
My reader group is where I spend a great deal of my on-line time. This group is filled with readers who have become friends and I'd like to take the time right now to thank them for their contributions to this book.

*

Betty Payton named Jacqueline (Jax) Masters
My husband Gene gave Dodge his last name - Sager (which happens to be my mother-in-law's maiden name)
Teresa Ellett Russ came up with the basic suspense angle of the story.
Gigi Boyd and Carol Stout came up with Gaige Vickers
Jen Hettrick named Axel and Nicky Ortiz gave Axel his last name Dunbar
Nicky Ortiz named Wyatt Lawson
Barb Keller named Hawk (Hawk's real name is Parker Everett)

Michele Smith and Terra Oenning named Josh Masters
Yvonne Cruz created the description for Axel Dunbar
Tami Czenkus created the description for Wyatt Lawson
Betty Payton created the description for Hawk
Kona Whitney and Barb Keller created the description for
Gaige Vickers
Terri Merkel created the description for Josh Masters
Vicky Brown named Guardwell Security
Barb Keller named Georgia Parks
Kimberly Johnson Ruiz named Pilar Masters
Kerry Harteker named the two EMTs Kevin and Jamie
Janeen Wagner Phillips named Francesca Santarino

A very special thank you to all of you for contributing to
Dodge and all of my stories. If you like to help create
characters, towns, companies and would like to join my
reader group on Facebook, PJ Fiala's Road Queens, join
us, we'd love to have you.

Of course, I would be remiss if I didn't thank my family
for all they do for me. From answering questions, to
helping with the daily chores, to just supporting me when
I'm down, thank you. I love you and couldn't do this
without you. Especially you, Gene. You make my life
complete.

1

BACK OFF

Let's stay in contact, join my newsletter so I can let you know about new releases, sales, promotions and more. https://www. subscribepage.com/pjfialafm

***

Dodge Sager entered the Copper Cup, his favorite hangout, highly alert and ready for action. Not his usual action, but work action. He was itching to find Mangus Santarino and follow him to his hiding place. He had an enormous gleaming pink diamond to retrieve from Mangus, the damned thief. Big Three Bounty Hunting's client, Guardwell, wanted the diamond back before its client raised all sorts of holy hell about it. That would ruin its reputation as being the only security transport company to never have anything stolen from them.

Glancing around he noted briefly the smattering of people in the bar. It wouldn't get busy til later which is probably why his informant told him Mangus would be here early. Taking a seat at the bar, the bartender, who was also his friend, Derek, jerked his head to the right but kept on wiping the bar down. "Usual?"

"Yeah." His eyes traveled in the direction of Derek's nod. In the back of the bar, where the booths were lined up along the wall for diners, sat a man wearing a baseball cap that boasted "Dodgers." Derek set his drink, which in reality was tea poured in a bourbon glass, in front of him on a napkin. Dodge met Derek's gaze and listened as his friend said, "Back booth, baseball cap, sexy brunette with him."

Lifting his drink to his lips, his eyes sought out the brunette with Mangus. Since Mangus was a married man, and this was not his wife according to the photographs he'd seen, he wondered what this was all about.

The dark-haired beauty threw her head back and laughed and Dodge was mesmerized by the sound. Damn woman had no idea what she was getting herself into.

Derek came back around after delivering drinks to other customers and laid a menu on the bar.

"Did the brunette come in with him?"

"Nope, she was here by herself. Began shooting pool with those guys in the back, kicked their asses, and then made her way to your friend."

Women! It was difficult to trust them in the best of circumstances. He'd learned that a long time ago.

The brunette stood from the booth and jutted her spectacular breasts out which not only got Mangus' attention but his, too. He may not trust women, but he sure did love to look, touch, and feel them. She picked up Mangus' glass and sauntered her sexy ass to the bar.

His eyes darted to Mangus and noted that he watched her ass as she walked away from him. Then he locked eyes with her. Dark shiny eyes pierced his. Her long dark lashes perfectly framed her almond shaped eyes and her full pink lips curved up slightly.

She set both hers and Mangus' glasses on the bar and purred, "Refill please."

She turned her head, her dark hair held hints of auburn and shined under the lights above the bar. "Little Mama, you have no idea what you're getting into with that man over there."

She laughed, then glared at him, which made the hair on the back of his neck stand-up, "Baby, you have no idea who I am or what I'm capable of."

Something plummeted into the bottom of his stomach at her look and the tone of her voice. Alarm bells rang in his head, then she interrupted his dark thoughts. "Mind your own business, Tarzan."

Derek set her drinks on the wooden bar top. She reached into her back pocket, pulled out a twenty-dollar bill, and handed it to him. "Keep it, I'll be back for more." She picked up her drinks, and without another glance in Dodge's direction her sexy ass moved away from him and back to Mangus.

Derek's chuckle caught his attention, the stupid dimple in his cheek that the women swooned over practically pointed at him and mocked him. "Man, she burned you good."

"She didn't burn me."

Derek laughed out loud then. "She so did, bro."

He walked to the other end of the bar to tend to customers leaving the view open to watch Mangus and the hot little mama with the sassy mouth.

Having Derek refill his "tea", he continued to look like a bored patron and tried not to stare at Mangus and his date. Suddenly, Mangus reached across the table and grabbed a handful of her gorgeous hair jerking her head back. He leaned forward and said something to her, jerked again on her hair, then released her. He sat back, the snarl on his face disgusting. The hot little mama frowned, then quick as the flip of a switch she smiled.

Dodge stood and made his way to the back of the bar and to Mangus. She didn't know what she was getting into. "That is no way to treat a lady."

The slow deliberate turn of Mangus' head almost turned his stomach. This was not a man who was used to being told what to do. "That so?" The question hung in the air like a thick cloud.

"Yes. That's so." He turned to the dark-haired woman and locked eyes with her. "You can leave here and I'll make sure he doesn't follow you."

She scoffed, then in a low measured tone said, "Mind. Your. Own. Business."

His brows furrowed and his back straightened. "Seriously?"

"Yes." Her lips barely moved.

Mangus took that moment to further her comments. "You need to go back to the bar and wallow in your pity party. You have no idea what we're all about."

Locking eyes with Mangus, he waited a beat, neither man looking away and neither one giving in to say anything further. The size up continued until the hot little mama broke the silence. "Go on and drown your sorrows, Tarzan, we're all good here."

His eyes slid to hers, held a beat, then he turned and stalked to the bar. Resuming his position, he lay his phone on the top of the bar in front of him and tapped his microphone button. Recording a message to himself for later, when he wrote up his report, his eyes scanned the room and noted two things. The men in the back that had been shooting pool with the crazy ass woman with Mangus had all left. And the bar began filling up with the after-work crowd.

Noting the time on his phone as 5:30 p.m., he prepared to settle in for a long night.

Then an opportunity presented itself. The hot little mama sauntered past the bar and toward the pool tables. The Copper Cup was shaped like an L with the booth Mangus occupied on one end and the pool table in the back at the other end. The bathrooms were also just past the pool table and then the backdoor. Once she was around the bend and out of sight to Mangus, and close to the backdoor, she stopped, looked over her right shoulder, and the come hither look she landed on him sent his libido into hyperdrive. Damn. Turning so quickly he half doubted she'd even looked at him, she proceeded out the backdoor.

His curiosity piqued, he glanced at his phone just as Derek stopped in front of him. "He looking at me?" He asked his friend. "Nope." Derek replied as he continued wiping the bar.

Nodding once, he pocketed his phone, stood, and followed the woman out the door to see where she'd gone.

The sun was still shining brightly in the sky, though sunset would be in three hours or so. Twisting the handle on the backdoor, he barely stepped completely out the door when he was hit in the stomach with an excruciating blow. Before his mind could comprehend what was happening, a leg wrapped around his and pulled knocking him on his ass. The air whooshed from his lungs and before he could catch his breath, the lovely woman with Mangus jumped on him, straddled his chest, and her small but strong hand gripped his throat and squeezed.

"I told you, twice, to back off. You need to leave me alone. Got it?"

Struggling to suck air into his lungs and assess the situation, she tightened her hold on his throat. "Hear me?"

Without enough air all he could muster was a weak, "Yeah," which wheezed from his lips in a futile attempt to answer. Her iron grip loosened, but her eyes continued to bore into his.

2

WE HAVE OPENINGS TO FILL

Pulling her motorcycle into the underground garage at GHOST headquarters, which is now home, Jax pulled into one of her two allotted parking spaces. Her sexy murdered out Jeep Wrangler sat in the other, looking almost evil with its darkened windows, black studded rims - well, black everything. She'd purchased it with her last bonus for a job well done. She and her twin brother, Josh, worked for GHOST, as had their father and older brother Jake, before them. Unfortunately, this job was both lucrative and dangerous. Their father was killed while undercover some twenty years ago, when she and Josh were around sixteen-years-old. Just three months ago, Jake had also been killed while undercover. By Victor Santarino's minions, the smarmy bastard. And though Victor was also now dead, his slimy brother, Mangus, was still alive and kicking and still running the family business of smuggling jewels and arms into the US. The jewels he usually cut up and resold, the arms were distributed around the world. It's the way Limitless did it, plus it's more lucrative.

She was taking this whole operation down if it was the last thing she ever did. To avenge her brother, she'd do anything.

Roughly pulling her helmet from her head and hanging it on the mirror of her bike, she pulled the hair band from her ponytail and scrubbed her fingers across her scalp to ease the itch from that damned helmet and hopefully some of her anger from that son of a bitch who caused her to lose Mangus at the Copper Cup.

Entering the elevator, she jabbed at the button that would take her up one floor, still below ground, which is where their group operated. This is where they met, organized, networked with other operatives, and researched. The rest of their work was out in the field.

The elevator doors opened and the muffled sounds from the shooting range on the opposite end of the house calmed her frazzled nerves. She loved the sound and smell of the shooting range. The feel of her gun as the hammer fired off a round and the acrid odor of gunpowder filled her nostrils, calmed her as much as a hot bath and a good book.

Instead of turning toward the shooting range, she walked down the hall and to the right to enter the computer lab. Her team lead, Gaige Vickers, sat at a computer, three monitors in front of him, all with documents and photographs arranged in a pattern that made sense to him. He worked in a methodical, organized manner that the others admired but didn't always appreciate.

"Hey Jax, look at this." He called over his shoulder.

"How did you know it was me?"

Without looking away from his computer screens, he

pointed to a fourth monitor, off to the right, which showed the GHOST garage on a video feed.

Taking a deep breath she walked to his left and sat at the empty chair, she should have known he was always watching.

"This is where I think Mangus is staying. It's low on the mountain where Victor's cabin is located. I think he has a hidden entry point at the base of the mountain and he's built a hideout inside. It's ingenious. And, since we have the bounty hunters living on the mountain across the river, we have a nice vantage point."

"Stop." She flipped her hair off her shoulder and took another breath. "Don't be impressed by him. He's an asshole of major proportions."

"That doesn't mean we can't learn from him."

The door swooshed open and Josh, along with the odor of gunpowder, filled her nostrils.

"Hey there, how did it go tonight?"

"Shitty." She turned on her chair to face him. He was the level headed one of the three the Masters' siblings. Meaning she and her brothers. "Some asshole thought Mangus was wrong for me and interrupted my plan. By the time I had him by the throat, literally, Mangus slipped out of the Copper Cup and I missed my chance at getting into his lair."

Gaige chuckled, "Well, I may have found his lair so you may still be able to get inside and not have to do it by making him think there's going to be a happy ending."

"The ending will be happy alright, but not for him." Leaning in she looked at the pictures Gaige had now distributed across the three screens. Roads leading to a mountain. Paths and trails leading to what seemed like nowhere. But nothing else.

Josh moved in closer and lay his hand on her right shoulder. He could calm her with just his hand on her shoulder. "So what we need to do now is go and explore where those paths lead to and, hopefully, we'll find out where Mangus is getting in and out of his hole in the mountain."

"Yep, we're on it. I have Axel, Wyatt, and Hawk on it now."

Gaige arched his back, then raised his arms to stretch them before turning in his chair and standing. "So, until they come back here and tell us how to get in, we need to relax and rest up. Get ready 'cause we'll be out there soon making our way inside."

He moved as gracefully as a man of his size could move. Gaige Vickers was over six feet tall, broad shoulders which he kept chiseled by lifting weights on a daily basis. And, even though she'd never get involved with him in a sexual way, she enjoyed watching him walk away. Call her crazy, but the man had a great ass.

"Good night you two, I'm off to hit the sack."

Both she and Josh said, "Night." She continued to watch him walk away until Josh interrupted her thoughts.

"So, some asshole ruined your plan?"

She looked into his dark brown eyes, so similar to her own and their lost brother Jake. Their half Hispanic heritage was strong in their complexions and coloring. Their mother, Pilar, gave them that. Their father was of Bohemian descent and gave them all the rest of their qualities. Strength, height, and agility. Both of her brothers were around six feet tall, she was average for a woman at five foot six, but about six inches taller than their mom.

"Yeah. So I lured him outside to make him understand

that I knew what I was doing and Mangus slipped out the front."

"Jax, make sure you're being careful. I can't lose you, too. It would kill Mama if you didn't come home from a mission."

"I'll be careful. I've just got to get him, Josh. I've got to make sure that man never sees the light of day again."

"Jax...killing him, if that's what you're implying, isn't our mission. And, you should probably keep those thoughts to yourself."

"I know what our mission is. But, MY mission is to make sure he's done. We both know he could run his enterprise from inside a prison, so the only way to stop it all is to wipe him off the face of the earth."

"And how do you think you'll do that alone?"

She stood, suddenly uncomfortable with his scrutiny, and crossed her arms in front of her. "I plan to drug him, dig through his files and things until I find what I need to complete our mission of finding out how and where Mangus is smuggling guns, into the country, how and where they are being repackaged, and where they are being distributed, so we can shut him down for our client. I seem to remember our client was very keen on, and I quote, "however we had to shut him down was fine with him". I'm fully aware of our mission, Josh."

They stood silently assessing each other when the door swished open again. "I forgot to tell you, we're meeting with the bounty hunters tomorrow night at 19:00 hours. They are all former military, Army, and they are all very good at their jobs. Two of them have had years of detective experience and one over twenty years of bounty hunting. I think we need to explore a partnership with them, and maybe we'll bring them on if we can all work together. Since we've lost Jake, Adams, and Branch, we have openings to fill.

3

THE MEETING

S aturday is meeting day. Since the inception of Big Three Bounty Hunting, the three partners, Ford, Lincoln, and Dodge had met to discuss the week's activities and dole out the work. Ford primarily found them the work since he had this business going before Lincoln and Dodge joined him, which meant he had the contacts. Lincoln, and especially Dodge, like being on the road.

Dodge pulled his truck up to the garage door of Ford's house on top of a mountain, owned by Ford and Megan, named Lynyrd Station on the Hill, where the views were breathtaking and the air was clean. Stepping from his truck he could hear the baby crying, and he twisted his neck to and fro to ease the tension. Shelby, Ford and Megan's three-month old daughter, had been colicky the past couple of weeks. He knew she was uncomfortable and Ford and Megan were doing all they could for Shelby, but dog gone dammit that crying got on his last nerve.

If he were being honest with himself, he'd say it was

because he'd had a shitty night last night. But, what did honesty ever get him?

He stepped up onto the deck that wrapped around the house so he could enter the house at the front. Sliding open one of the glass doors the volume of Shelby's crying rose another decibel. He took a deep breath and let it out. Quiet as a mouse, not that anyone would hear him over the crying, he made his way across the room to the coffee pot, opened a cupboard, and helped himself to a cup. Ford knew he was here, his security system would have alerted him as soon as Dodge began coming up the driveway.

Taking his mug to the sofa, he glanced at the coffee table and noted there weren't any folders for he and Lincoln filled with work orders. His brows furrowed as a myriad of thoughts about why this would be swirled through his head.

No work.

Unlikely.

Ford hadn't had time to pull them together.

Highly likely, lately, with a new baby at home.

Walking to the glass doors he looked out at the view and took another deep breath as the peaceful scenery acted as a bit of a balm to his mood. That and the warm coffee in his mug.

The crying softened just as his friend and partner, Lincoln walked around the corner of the house and silently opened the glass door. Dodge stepped back to allow him entry. Shelby wailed out again and Lincoln winced. The two men said nothing but greeted each other with a nod and a handshake.

Lincoln walked to the coffee pot while Dodge turned and sat on the sofa to wait for his partners. Shelby's crying subsided, and Ford emerged from the baby's room looking bedraggled and tired.

Softly he greeted them. "Morning guys. Meg had to run down the mountain to get something for Shelby's tummy at the pharmacy and I'm on dad duty until she gets home. Sorry."

Dodge replied first. "No problem. Will she be gone long?"

Lincoln chuckled. "Subtle much?"

Shaking his head, Dodge brought his coffee to his lips and decided to let his caffeine work a bit before saying anything else.

Luckily, Ford understood and saved him from replying. "No, she's already on her way back." Just as Ford had the words out of his mouth the security system beeped and Ford commented, "She's coming up the drive now."

"No work this week?" Lincoln asked before Dodge got the chance.

"Here's what I'd like to discuss." Ford poured his own coffee but before he could continue, the door to the garage opened and Meghan walked in with a little white bag from the pharmacy in town. He leaned in and kissed his gorgeous wife, she waved to Lincoln and Dodge, then went into Shelby's room with the medicine and closed the door.

"Okay, so as I said, there's something we need to discuss." Ford continued. "We're not running out of work but we now have two bondsmen who haven't paid us. Rumor has it a third will be having issues paying us as well. This on top of the fact we're killing ourselves, so we need to discuss expansion of the company."

Dodge shook his head, "That makes no sense. Clients aren't paying us so we should expand?"

Ford sat on the chair at a right angle to the sofa where Dodge and Lincoln sat, set his cup on the coffee table, and folded his hands together between his knees as he leaned his forearms on his thighs. "I got a call from Gaige Vickers, team lead for GHOST. Rory told us they are in town, and they are after the Santarinos' activities, much like we are. Different targets though. Our client, Guardwell wants the pink diamond back and it told us Mangus Santarino stole it from them; they want the whole operation. GHOST has offered to give us a shot at working with them to see if we're a fit." He looked up and his face showed worry. "I never have to worry about money again, guys. You know that, but I can't retire. I've thought about it. Meg and I have talked about it, and you guys know just these past few months of finding the work and managing the business isn't my cup of tea. Now we have clients not paying and I'm wondering why we'd keep doing business this way when we could try to work for GHOST, get paid, well I might add, and enjoy what we do." He took a sip of coffee and Dodge let that sink in for a minute.

Then he blurted out. "How well?"

"Very well. GHOST is largely hired by the US Government. Rory thinks they're getting Mangus from a private client who might be an arms dealer that the Santarino brothers screwed over, his daughter was caught up in it and killed, but he's not positive. They're undercover most of the time, they're experienced, and they have equipment that would make Jared Timm piss himself with glee."

Now that sounded fantastic. One of Dodge's dreams was to be able to pay off his parents' house for their anniversary. He was close, but if clients stopped paying, that would halt his progress. His mind floated over money, equipment, and working with experienced operatives. A dream come true for sure. He rubbed his thumb over his bottom lip and began thinking of the possibilities.

Lincoln began asking questions. "It'll affect Skye since she won't have a job any longer. Again. And, how often would we be gone?"

Dodge looked at Ford as he shrugged. "I think the way they operate is by round table. A job comes in, they discuss it among the team and a decision is made. If you want to stay close to the home front, I'd bet concessions can be made as long as they don't harm the team. They run a clean operation and they work together as a tight unit. I won't lie though, the reason they're interested in us is because they've recently lost three operatives in the field, one of them Jake Masters, the operative Skye saw murdered in her parents' field. It can be dangerous."

Lincoln rubbed the back of his neck before replying, "I'll need to talk to Skye first Ford, it affects both of us."

"I'm aware and wouldn't expect anything less from you."

Ford turned to him then, "Dodge, what are you thinking?"

"I'm interested. But, I'm afraid I'm in a bit of a mood today so I don't want to be rash. When do we have to let them know?"

"They've asked us to come to their headquarters here in Lynyrd Station at 19:00 hours to talk about how it all works and what we'd be doing. We'll also meet their operatives and see how we get along."

He and Lincoln nodded then Ford changed the topic of conversation. "So, here's where we're at with Mangus and Limitless. It appears that when Limitless was in business, before the feds came in and shut them down, Mangus hated the arms dealing. He knew Victor was doing it, he knew Victor placed hits on people and largely ran on the wrong side of the law. He looked the other way as long as Victor was around to deal with it. Not anymore. He's also not innocent. He's continued with his jewelry and art theft, but he's stepped it up because money is tight now. He's more than likely a bit more desperate and that means, more deadly. So tell us what happened last night and if you saw Mangus."

He filled them in on what happened, his anger at missing Mangus leave growing in the pit of his stomach once again. He had to take deep breaths to keep his temper in check.

They left their meeting, and Dodge's job was to read through some reports that Jared Timm, their buddy from the Army and resident computer hacker/conspiracy theorist had sent over to Ford. Jared didn't come cheap, but he always came through for them. His spider networks were the stuff that would make the government cringe. So to hear Ford say that he'd be impressed with GHOST's computer network and equipment was saying something.

*

By 19:00 hours he and Lincoln were once again at Ford's to meet up for their interview. He felt jittery for some reason and brushed it off as being too sedentary today, reading up on Mangus Santarino and some possibilities on where he's living at the moment.

They agreed to take separate vehicles so they could each go their own way after the meeting. He followed behind his friends' trucks down the mountain, telling himself to calm down and buck up. He was good at his job. They all were and fucking GHOST would be damn lucky to have them on board. The threat of death didn't scare him off after three tours in Iraq, and then working as a cop then a detective for twenty years at home in Alabama.

They drove through town and Ford pulled into the driveway of a beautifully kept Southern mansion. The wrought iron gates were ornate and massive. A light on the security box blinked, and flashed before the gate opened inward to allow them entry. The estate came into full view and the enormous white home, complete with a large covered porch and baskets of flowers hanging in several places greeted them. It looked like a traditional Southern mansion you'd find in Savannah, Georgia. Then Dodge's mind tuned to what in the hell they were doing here!

He watched as his two friends parked and exited their trucks, both of them looking in awe at the overly large home they stood before.

He followed suit and the instant he closed his truck door a man stepped from inside and greeted them. "Welcome Big Three. Come on in and I'll introduce you to the crew that's here. I still have three guys out in the field."

They stepped up onto the porch and he shook hands as they each told him their names. "My name is Gaige Vickers and I'm the team lead for GHOST. Come on in."

They followed him inside and awe wasn't a strong enough word. The dark wooden floors gleamed from the light cast by the chandeliers above. The wall coverings were of high quality damask in muted tones of mauve and light greens. The curved staircase with its gleaming dark mahogany banister and white marble stairs were impressive and that was saying a lot since this entire place was impressive.

Gaige stopped and looked around as if seeing it again for the first time. "It's incredible, isn't it?"

Ford spoke first, "It certainly is. I'm stunned and impressed as I wasn't expecting anything like this for the headquarters of a government agency."

"Ah, well, that's because we aren't government. The government is our primary client, but we are completely independent. We do have some private clients. The government and our clients pay us well. We do things the government can't because of regulations or appearances. If we're caught by any authority, the government will deny any knowledge or working relationship with us. But, someone high up signs a check and we're golden."

Dodge finally found his voice. "So, why this? It's impressive for certain, but it hardly allows you to blend."

Gaige laughed then and Dodge begrudgingly thought the women probably swooned for Gaige Vickers. He was tall and broad with the dark blond hair and chiseled jaw he heard them chatter over during his military and police days. "We're not trying to blend. This house was available when we came to town. We didn't have that much work to do to it to update it. We hired an interior designer and she completed the house to return it to its natural origins, but with us in mind. Her team swooped in and had us up and running in no time. It also offered us what we really need and that's room to spread out, work out, and practice. We have two floors below this one. One is our main head-quarters area complete with workout facility, computer lab, gun range, conference room, and medical unit. The lowest level houses our vehicles. We're bulletproof in case we're found out, and our lower levels also serve as a bunker should the worst happen and we have to be locked down for any length of time."

"Wow." It came out of his mouth before he could catch himself. The last thing Dodge wanted was to come in here and seem like an overly impressed teenager, but damned if he wasn't doing just that now.

Gaige chuckled again and continued. "Come on down and meet some of the team."

Dodge followed Gaige down a corridor which held four wall niches, each one with a light shining down on a bronze statue of soldiers on horseback. He recognized George Washington and he assumed one was Robert E. Lee, but didn't have time to read the inscriptions on any of them.

Gaige waived a security card in front of a small, deep bronze panel on the wall, next to a door that to the outside appeared to be a bedroom door, five horizontal panels, painted white. But inside stood an elevator. A large elevator. Each of them stepped inside and Gaige pushed a button, the doors closed and their descent began.

Reaching the floor just below them, the readout on the panel said, Conf., the doors opened and he ushered them across the hall and through a glass door. This level was the complete opposite of the first floor. Glass doors, and frosted glass windows gleamed down the hallway. Lighting from the rooms lit the hallway and movement could be seen behind the glass but nothing distinguishable. They entered the room and the array of computer equipment was staggering. One wall held various monitors and screens, some of them on, some not. Computers lined up along that wall, had their screen savers showing slide shows of various designs. Dodge assumed each team member had their own computer and screen saver.

"This is the computer lab in case you didn't guess by now. Generally, I run the computers, but Josh over here is no slouch on that front, either." He turned to the man he called Josh and addressed him. "Josh Masters, meet the

Big Three, Ford Montgomery, Lincoln Winter, and Dodge Sager."

Josh shook hands with each of them and they were ushered to a conference table. Josh said, "Jax will be down in a minute. In the meantime, what can we get you guys to drink?"

"Water is great, if you don't mind." Dodge replied and his friends nodded in agreement. As Josh brought bottled water from a refrigerator and set them down in front of each of them, the door whooshed open and he damned near spat the large gulp of water he'd just poured into his mouth.

4

OH, HELL NO.

"Oh, hell no. This cannot be them. No fucking way, Gaige."

She'd gotten their attention, all of them, and she meant to nip this in the bud right the fuck now. "This is the asshole who made me lose Mangus last night. Acted all Tarzan, me man, you woman crap and when I had to straighten him out, Mangus got away."

"Tarzan? Are you fucking kidding me with this shit? I was there watching Mangus and you were in over your fucking head. Because of you, I lost him."

"You don't know the first thing about what I'm capable of. Typical man assuming I can't handle myself. I believe I showed you how capable I am when I had you on the ground and was sitting on top of you, you fucking Neanderthal."

He glanced at his partners with a look of irritation and frustration on his face. Handsome though it was. She was too pissed to do anything but stop this partnership from happening.

His words were measured when he addressed his friends. "I am so sick of being called a Neanderthal. What the fuck?"

She noted with a bit of pleasure that both of his friends grinned but didn't say a word.

"So, I'm not the only one to notice. Ha!" She practically barked she was so friggin' mad.

Gaige interrupted their argument. "Okay, that's enough from both of you. Let's all sit down and discuss this."

What? Now they were going to sit and discuss it? Why in the hell would they do that? She didn't want to work with someone who thought of her as the dumb little woman. She'd had far too much of that her entire damned life, especially in the military. No one gave her the credit she'd earned. First in her class in AIT - 35M Human Intelligence Collector, toughest damned man or woman in her whole unit. Best grades. Highest score on the gun range - sharpshooter status. Just when life seemed to finally reward her for her accomplishments with money and prestige, here she goes again. Damn.

She stood, stiff and solid, and watched as all the men sat and looked her way. Josh got her attention, "Jax, let's discuss this. 35M, remember?"

Her eyes locked with his, and he smiled. Got her every time.

She raised her eyebrows, but sat at the table and put on her interrogation hat to show these cavemen she was a force to be reckoned with. Yeah, that's what she'd do.

Gaige started in, "So, Jax, it appears you've met Dodge Sager." He motioned toward the one called Dodge with his hand, then continued on around the table. "Ford Montgomery and Lincoln Winter. This is Jax

Masters. She and Josh are Agent Jake Masters' twin siblings."

Ford addressed her first. "It's nice to meet you Jax and please accept our condolences for your brother's loss." He glanced at Lincoln, "Lincoln's wife, Skye, was the witness to his murder and it's haunted her since."

Her eyes sought Lincoln's and the steely gray of his eyes showed her without words the seriousness of that statement. "I'm sorry for your loss. I can't imagine." He offered. Glancing to Josh, to include him in the sentiment.

He stopped then and she could tell he was affected by her brother's death. She wanted nothing more than to question him endlessly about the final moments of her brother's life. What happened, exactly. Did those bastards make him suffer? Did they make him beg? All the things that kept her awake at night. She wanted to know it all. Then again, Josh kept telling her she didn't want to know the details. "Once you hear it, Jax, you can't unhear it. Think about it long and hard." He'd told her countless times.

Dodge looked at Josh, his lips turned down, then his eyes landed on her. "Sorry for your loss."

Gaige continued. "Okay, so here's where we're at. We have three operatives out in the field now combing a mountain where we think Mangus is hiding. It's out where Victor had his cabin, and rather than being high up on that mountain, we think he's hiding in it." He stood and walked to his computer and pulled up the picture he'd shown her earlier. Tapping a few keys, a large screen rolled down from the ceiling and the same picture projected onto the screen in front of the conference table.

Trees and brush grown thick on the mountain side and three snaky roads, more like dirt trails than roads, disappeared into the brush. The roads were not well used and there didn't seem to be the appearance of a driveway, doorway, or entrance in the pictures.

"This is where we think Mangus is hiding." He pointed to an area at the center of the screen. "We had a drone flying over the area the past few days because Mangus' car had been seen in the area by one of our informants. We caught footage from a distance, saw him turn onto this road here," He pointed to an area low on the screen where the county road met the dirt road. "Then he disappeared. Since none of us believe even Mangus Santarino can actually disappear, we think he has a secret passageway into the mountain and his lair inside."

Gaige looked around the room at both teams assembled together. Dodge spoke first and she tightened her jaw when he spoke. "We have a client, Guardwell, who tells us Mangus stole a raw pink diamond weighing in at an impressive 162.5 carats which disappeared en route from Johannesburg to the United States. The diamond has been described as "of unbelievable clarity and extremely rare" and has an estimated value of well over thirty-five million dollars. We need to recover the diamond before Mangus cuts it up and sells it off before you can shut him down. Our client's reputation is on the line."

Josh spoke up and she damned near fell off her chair at what he said. "We should be able to work together on this. Basically, we want the same thing. Our client on this is a billionaire who lost a daughter because of the Santarinos and he wants the information about how the jewels and arms, if there are still some in the mix, are being smuggled. But, more than anything, he wants that operation finished. So he's hired us to do what the government is incapable of doing before he gets away. We want to know where he's smuggling from and how. Then we want to know how he's moving product out of the US. Finally, we shut him and his operation down and get a check."

Slowly she twisted her neck to stare at her brother. When he refused to meet her eyes she knew this was a losing battle. Even her brother wanted to work with these guys. Un-friggin'-believable!

Gaige took the lead, "Okay, then I think we need to determine if we want to do this. My vote is yes; we give it a try."

Ford chimed in, "I'm in."

Lincoln continued. "I'm in, if we can agree moving forward on a strategy for taking jobs that will allow me and my wife to have some time together."

Gaige nodded. "Taking a mission is discussed and evaluated and if we're manned up enough, you can sit back and help out here in the computer lab or elsewhere on the compound that won't put you in the field. We like having two full crews, so there's usually no issue."

Gaige looked to Dodge then. "I'm in."

Dodge turned his head and locked eyes with hers and damn if she didn't see challenge in them. Okay, if that was how he was going to play it, so would she.

"Jax?" Gaige prompted.

"I'm in." She managed, though it almost stuck in her throat.

Gaige cocked his head as he looked her way. When their eyes met his brows rose. She smiled and added. "I think I can show these guys how capable a woman is in the field and impress the shit out of them."

Josh elbowed her gently. "That you will, sis. I'm in too."

"I'm team lead and that means, I'll direct operations

and teams. When our field ops come back we'll get their votes too, so you guys will need to meet them." His phone rang and he held up his forefinger as he pulled his phone from his back pocket. "Vickers."

The group chatted quietly with each other and she begrudgingly had to admit they did seem decent. Respectable and even knowledgeable. Damn. There was a bit of hope in her that they wouldn't like each other and this would be a short-term partnership, but it seemed that Josh enjoyed talking with them.

Hanging up his phone Gaige continued, "In the meantime, I just got intelligence that there's a meeting going on at a house in Lynyrd Station and Mangus Santarino was seen entering the house about a half hour ago. We need to go to the house and see what we can find out about this meeting. It might give us some valuable information on his operations. Jax and Dodge, you two can work on this one together.

"In the meantime, Ford and Lincoln, Josh will show you around the compound. We have a weapons room, shooting range, elevator to the parking garage and spare bedrooms upstairs if you need to crash in between shifts or jobs. Once you're finished, I'll give you the passcodes to come and go. By then, hopefully, Axel, Wyatt, and Hawk will be back and you can meet."

Lincoln glanced at Dodge and she had to bite the inside of her cheek at the grin he turned on Dodge. In turn, Dodge lifted his middle finger and flipped off both of his friends who chuckled as they stood to follow Josh from the room.

Gaige stepped to his computer, hit a couple buttons which raised the screen into the ceiling and the printer began purring and spitting out paper. He pulled them from the printer and brought them to the table. "Here's the address and information on the owner of the house. You two figure out how to manage this. You can do this."

Gaige left the room and silence filled the air. Then Dodge took the papers looked through them, nodded once then said. "I can drive if you like." He lay the papers on the table and shoved them her way. Glancing at the address, she repeated it in her head a couple of times.

Letting her breath out slowly, she bit the inside of her bottom lip, then nodded. "Sure, I'll just run up to my room and grab a couple of things. I'll meet you out front."

Silently, they took the elevator together and on the main floor she pointed to the front door. "I'll meet you outside."

She watched as Dodge stepped out of the front door, then she quickly ran to the elevator and pushed the button that said 'Garage'. Biting her bottom lip, she knew this was wrong and certainly no way to treat a teammate, but she needed to show them she could do this on her own and keep Dodge from assuming she was the "little woman." She needed them to see that she was an operative just like the rest of them.

As soon as the elevator doors slid open she ran to her motorcycle, shoved her helmet on her head, and exited out the back entrance. Keeping the rpms on her bike low so she didn't make a lot of noise, she eased out onto the street and lost herself in traffic before she could be seen from the house. She repeated the address in her head over and over as she traveled along the busy streets in town. Both sides of Main Street were lined with cars. It was Saturday night and the pool league was in full swing. As she passed the Copper Cup, the music from the jukebox spilled out of the door as a patron left the building and the notes of a country song briefly filled the air.

Turning onto Fourth Street, she parked at the end of the block and walked to the house. She could do this all by herself.

5

JAX!

L ooking around the exterior of the home he had to admit again, it was impressive. This actually could be a great partnership, if Jax could reign in her attitude and her emotions. Typical woman to get all emotional over little things.

Damned women!

Climbing in his truck, he stopped and turned his head as the sound of a motorcycle sounded in the distance. Sounded fantastic with the low grumble of the pipes. He'd like to be on his bike right now, the weather was perfect for a ride. Then maybe the tension in his shoulders, which started last night, would ease. There was nothing like getting outside, letting the wind hit your face, and feeling the rumble under you as the growl of your pipes erased any other sounds.

He waited a few minutes, checked the time on his phone, and waited another couple of minutes. The growing irritation did nothing for the tightness in his shoulders so he stepped from his truck and walked to the house. Entering the front door, he was again struck with the opulence of this place. Everything was immaculate. Not sure if he should make his way upstairs to find Jax or head back down to the conference room he was stuck by indecision. Then the voices of Ford, Lincoln, and Gaige carried from the back of the house, somewhere behind the staircase and he decided to head in that direction.

Entering the kitchen his impression was again ramped up at the gleaming white marble countertops and the dark wood floor. His friends sat at the kitchen table, which looked more like a large wooden dining table, tucked into a nook at the far side of the kitchen. Gaige's brows furrowed. "I thought you and Jax left for the house where Mangus was seen."

He shrugged. "I'm waiting for her to come back down so we can leave."

Gaige's jaw tightened and his shoulders pulled back. "I'll go find her. Sit down and relax, I'll just be a minute."

He sat uneasily and captured Lincoln's eyes. "I don't know, man, this might be more of a pain than it's worth. The last time I waited for a woman to get ready, I was married to her and we all know how that turned out."

Ford leaned in, his forearms on the table. "We haven't even given this a try yet, Dodge. Let's at least do that. Just talking to Gaige and Josh, I'm impressed with their operation."

Lincoln nodded and continued. "It's quite the set up here. I can see a long career with these guys and this unit. I like how they do things."

He exhaled, "All but one."

Ford leaned forward, "Right and on another note, did you catch that their client is a billionaire? Rory had the impression it was a disgruntled arms dealer. I'll have to give him a call and see if he has changed that opinion."

Lincoln responded quietly. "I wondered about that, too."

Gaige entered the kitchen. "Okay, I have to apologize, which I don't like doing, but it appears Jax left on her own. "I'm sorry, Dodge, this is not how we do things."

Shaking his head, he stood and began walking toward the front door. "She seems a bit self-centered if you ask me. I'll head out there."

He heard Gaige apologizing again to his partners, "Sorry guys. It appears there will be an adjustment period."

Hopping up into his truck he decided all bets were off on this one. She wanted to play this game, he was in. The gloves were off. Keeping himself in check with this woman was going to test him in every way imaginable. She'd ducked out on him and dammit, he wanted to know where that damned diamond was before she blew this whole thing out of the water. Going off half-cocked like she did proved to him she wasn't a team player.

Focusing on relaxing his jaw as he neared the house at the East end of Lynyrd Station, he rolled some of the intelligence through his head. Four people were seen entering the house around an hour ago. That meant a minimum of five people inside, could be more, depending on the number of occupants. Since one of the guests was Mangus Santarino, according to the informant working with GHOST, he had to assume they were all armed and on high alert to any action, that meant danger.

Closer to the house, he saw a full front porch lit only by the light coming from the large window on the right side. Curtains were drawn and no visible movement could be seen. Assuming they were watching the street, he didn't want to slow too much and draw attention so he continued by, watching for movement.

At the end of Fourth Street he saw a lone motorcycle parked on the street, a black helmet perched on the right mirror. No other vehicles were on the street and the overhead light directly across the street was burnt out. Convenient. Driving past the motorcycle he parked in front of it and quietly exited his truck. Making his way in the dark to the bike, he felt around the motor and noted that it was still warm. Making a mental note to admire the wicked looking murdered out Night Rod special, he set off toward the house at an easy pace, wanting to look like a man out for a walk.

One house away he noted movement at the back of the house in question and wondered if his eyes were playing tricks on him. Deciding to walk past the house and duck in around the neighboring house to the right, he trained his peripheral vision on movement and his ears on sounds.

Ignoring the adrenaline creeping into his muscles and his rapidly beating heart, he passed the house and inwardly smiled to himself when he noticed the neighbor had a large boxwood hedge between the two homes. Darting behind the hedge on the neighbor's side, he inhaled deeply and stood motionless for a moment hoping the neighbor didn't have a dog.

When no sound came, he looked for a break in the hedge that would allow him a visual if not an entry point to the subject house.

Finding a decent sized opening he looked through the

hedge to the backdoor of the house, and from the corner of his eye he saw movement. Zeroing in on the movement he clamped his jaw together, gritted his teeth, and silently swore as he saw a small woman jack-rabbiting across the backyard. Jax!

6

YOU GOT A PLAN?

J ax ducked behind the house through the neighbor to the left's backyard. No fences in this area was a boon, she didn't want to encounter a dog and all the barking and bull that came along with dealing with it.

Slowly edging her way past four cars in the driveway, she lay her hand on the hood of each car to feel how warm it was. The last one in the driveway was warmest, and that made perfect sense. She'd guestimate that it had been here around twenty minutes. Making her way to a window at the back of the house, she eased herself onto the edging, peering into the window she saw the kitchen, dirty pots and pans laying around, plates with leftover food, as if dinner had just concluded. Looking farther into the house through the kitchen doorway she could see the legs of someone sitting in an armchair, but not who. Easing herself off the edging she stood on, she quietly made her way around to another window on the east side. This window showed an office or study with papers strewn around, and a laptop with the lid closed on the desk.

Once again moving around the house to the west side she found the window she wanted to look in, but worried she'd be seen. Thinking it best to find another window, which might be less visible to her, she continued around the front of the house, keeping her back to the wall and her profile as small as possible. Not ideal, but she hoped it would give her a vantage point to see how many people were in the living room. Perhaps there'd be a place where the curtains didn't cover the full window. When she got back to the compound she'd look closer at the dossier Josh had given them and see who owned the house and for how long. She needed to stop this asshole, Santarino, from ever hurting another person. Her brother Jake deserved to have his death not be in vain. If those bitches married to these men were here in the states, she'd find a way to get to them, too.

Noticing headlights panning the street, she ran behind the house once again and continued to look for a way into the house. The basement windows were small, but so was she. If she could get one opened, she could enter the house and listen from a hidden vantage point.

Creeping to the side of the house, she tested the first basement window and noted that it was loaded with bugs, dirt, and looked as though no one ever used it. Perfect. Pulling a pocketknife from her back pocket, she ran it around the window seal, hoping the latch was a flip latch. Pocketing her knife, she pried the window with her fingers.

A large firm hand wrapped around her mouth, while steely arms picked her up and carried her to the back of the house. She kicked at her captor, clawed at the hand that held her firmly in place, and squirmed with all her might. Getting her mind adjusted to her own safety, she tried focusing on where she was being taken. She opened her eyes while continuing to thrash, watching the side of the house disappear around a corner as she was dragged behind the garage.

"Shush, you'll get us caught." The familiar voice scolded her in a whisper.

She froze, gathering her wits before kicking back and connecting with her captor's shin.

"Fucking hell, stop it." He quietly commanded.

His arm tightened around her waist and the palm covering her mouth increased its grip over her lips, sealing her nose in the process. As the fear from lack of breath began to crawl up her body, her stomach lurching wildly, her vision dimming to darkness. She tried screaming, but sound was muffled at best. Her lungs burned as the lack of oxygen encompassed them.

"I'll let you go when you promise two things. One, you'll shut your mouth and two, you'll stop kicking at me."

She nodded as much as could with the iron grip holding her against the solid wall of muscle behind her. "Oh, and there's a third thing. You'll start treating me like one of your team members and I'll vouch for you with Gaige. He's not very happy with you right now."

She closed her eyes and willed her body to calm. She felt his chest expand and deflate as his grip eased up but didn't move away completely. "I mean it Jax, you got me?"

Able to nod, she did, and his hand peeled away from her mouth, but the iron band around her waist never relaxed.

"Now, you're going to calmly and quietly tell me what you've been up to and what we're facing in there. But first,

I remind you that we have a dual mission here. We need to recover the diamond before this operation gets shut down. Got it?"

Taking her time to fill her lungs and release a few times, she stared straight ahead where the yard was dimly lit from the neighbor to the right's backyard light shining through the trees.

Her heartbeat began to slow to normal, "Got it." Pausing to check her temper, she continued. "All I've managed so far is to see into the kitchen and office windows." Peering around the corner of the garage she nodded in the direction of the window. "I was going to crawl into the basement and see if I could hear anything from down there when I was so rudely interrupted."

Feeling the chuckle deep in his chest, she marveled that he was able to remain so quiet while seemingly so amused by her. Blinking rapidly to keep her irritation in check she let out a long breath and told herself to behave. Figuring she'd have enough to deal with at the compound and knowing she'd want to die if she lost this job and the ability to avenge Jake's death, she bit the inside of her cheek.

The warm breath in her ear and the low growl of his voice actually caused her nipples to pucker, which also irritated the shit out of her. "I may have just saved your life. If you'd been caught in there, who knows what they'd do to you."

Her nose actually wrinkled on its own. "If we're going to be a 'team' you'd better start realizing that I've been with GHOST for close to fourteen years. Before that, I had a distinguished career in the Army for twelve years. And, among other specialties, I've attained sharpshooter status. I've never been captured; I've never failed a mission. But there could be a first time that I've wounded a partner if you keep this crap up."

His arm loosened and he stepped back from her. She could hear his breathing. It seemed as though he was trying to get himself under control.

She turned to stare him down, but dammit, it was dark back here behind the garage. The creaking of a door opening and low pitched voices came from the house. Silently turning to peek around the corner of the garage, she watched as two men stepped onto the small landing at the backdoor. They shook hands and the taller man with reddish hair softly said something to the dark-haired shorter man. The darker man nodded then stepped off the landing and disappeared around the corner. A door opened in one of the cars in the driveway, then closed just before the car started up. The headlights panned through the trees and the low rumble of the motor floated away as the car and driver left her view and her hearing.

Dodge's deep voice then whispered, "You got a plan?"

7

WELL, FUCK ME.

His anger had surged to boiling when he saw her trying to pry a basement window open. He'd come up behind her without her hearing him. What in the hell did GHOST need her for? No one should have been able to sneak up on her if she'd been paying attention to her surroundings.

Grabbing her and dragging her to the back of the house, he managed to get her behind the garage without making enough noise to wake the dead. Once he got her attention and she knew who he was, she stiffened but at least stopped scratching and kicking the hell out of him.

Letting her go, he said, "You're way off base, Jax. What if I was someone who could kill you? You've got to get your head in this game and stop trying to dump me." She spun around and glared at him, as much as she could in the dark, but he could see the whites of her eyes and he saw when they narrowed.

"We've got a mission here, Jax. The diamond first, then stopping the Santarino business second. Are you with me or not?"

He heard her intake a long breath, then let it out before finally responding. "Yes, I'm with you." It wasn't quite spat out, but it was close. Maybe she was warming up to him.

The backdoor opened again and another tall man, wearing black cargo pants stepped out of the house and looked around the backyard. They were crouched behind the garage watching around the corner in silence as he looked around. A third man stepped out, shook hands with the first man and then said, "I'll see you 'down there' next week, Ian." He jumped in his truck and left.

Dodge leaned close and whispered in Jax's ear, "We need to find out where 'down there' is."

She nodded, turned to look at him and a few things struck him. She smelled amazing. Her dark eyes practically sparkled and held so much in them. Intelligence and confidence, a heady combination. Then she replied, "Yep, and I know how to do it."

After the truck left and the redhead named Ian stepped inside Dodge whispered, "How?"

She pointed to a window on the far west side of the house. "That's an office. If we can wait out this group leaving, I'll slip into that window and steal the laptop on the desk. We can have Gaige work his magic on it and see if we can get anything from it. A location would be amazing, anything else, would be phenomenal."

"Jax..."

" Do. Not. Say. It. I'm capable Dodge. I've done this hundreds of times. Let me do my job."

She whispered it, but her determination was clear. He took in a breath to tell her that maybe he should be the one but she continued before he got the chance. "You want me to trust you, you need to trust me."

Good point. "Okay. In the meantime, we're stuck here until the crowd clears."

As if he summoned him, the backdoor opened and they both stopped talking and again peered around the back of the garage to watch the same red-headed man usher another guest from inside. They spoke softly, shook hands, and the other man left. As soon as his car cleared the driveway, Jax pulled a small device from her back pocket, turned a switch on it, and a light green glow lit then slowly dimmed out. Quickly glancing at the house to make sure no one saw the light, he turned back to her only to see her hold her finger to her lips as a way to silence him.

His brows furrowed, but before he could say anything the backdoor opened once more and this time the redhead stepped out with Mangus. Jax held the device out in front of her and watched the two men talk. Mangus turned and left. By Dodge's count that left only one other person in the house with the red-haired man if the pattern of one person per car held true.

He listened as Mangus' car door closed, his car started, and the headlights shone on the garage, then panned the backyard as he pulled out of the driveway. They were once again in the dark. He nudged Jax, then pointed around the side of the garage, letting her know he was going around to check. She nodded.

He stood and made his way quietly around the back and side of the garage and peered along the far west side. It was clear of debris but high weeds would make noise if he chose to walk along to get a look from that vantage point. Crouching down he slowly made his way to Jax, who sat still as stone. He watched her for a moment and had to admit to himself she was pretty good at this. She didn't seem scared or whiny, but confident and actually rather excited.

Still holding the device in her hand she again touched her finger to her lips then pointed to the back of the house. The last guest was finally leaving. When he looked back to Jax she actually smiled. That's when a couple of things hit him at once. She smelled fucking amazing and her eyes emanated intelligence and self-assurance. It was heady. His heart hammered in his chest as a weird excitement raced through his body.

The car left the driveway and they both ducked back as the headlights panned the yard. Looking back to the house, the kitchen light went off shrouding the back of the house in darkness. Tapping Jax's shoulder he pointed to the house, then curved his hand as if motioning that he was checking the front of the house. She smiled at him again, pulled another small device from her pocket that looked to be about the size of a cigarette lighter. Nodding, she hustled to the back of the house without a word. He saw her holding the smaller unit up to the house as she walked around the perimeter slowly, staying close to the outside walls to be undetected. He needed to find out what some of her cool little toys were.

He watched her disappear around the front of the house and he felt rather the fool 'cause he didn't know what he should do now. Deciding to check the front of the house, as he'd meant to do before, he silently made his way across the distance to the house. Planting himself to the wall, he saw Jax coming from the opposite direction and to him.

"No security system. I should be able to open the window without an alarm going off, that's one good thing." She turned the second device she'd pulled from her pocket and showed him the low light screen. It said, "No security system detected."

She tucked it in her pocket after he'd read it, then pulled up the second device she had in her hand. She once again held her finger to her lips, turned toward the office window and slowly ran the device along the top of the window. As she reached the middle of the top of the window, a soft click was heard. She froze and peered inside and so did he.

His eyes had long ago adjusted to the darkness and he could see into the office from the moonlight that filtered in. Just as Jax had said, there sat the laptop on the corner of the desk. After a few moments she began pushing on the bottom of the window to open it. Finally, something he could do. He tapped her shoulder and she stepped aside to allow him to move in front of it. He slowly lifted the window, grateful that it made no sound and that it wasn't an old painted shut contraption they'd have to wrestle with. The instant he had the window open, Jax hopped up on the sill, lifted her left knee, and silently hoisted herself inside. She was agile, and as stealthy as anyone he'd ever seen. Quietly picking up the laptop, she checked for a cord to make sure it wasn't plugged in, then handed it out the window to him. Taking it from her, he absently held his hand out to help her from inside only to see the quick shake of her head before sitting on the sill, twisting on her ass, and quietly jumping out.

She reached for the laptop and pointed to the window conveying without words that he should close it. The thought flitted through his mind that he was only good to do heavy lifting and grunt work. Which also called to mind that she had done this a few times before, she knew exactly what she was doing.

Once the window was closed, they silently walked across the backyard and out to the sidewalk from one of the neighbor's houses. Keeping their pace steady so as not to call attention to themselves they walked without talking. As they reached the motorcycle and his truck it dawned on him who that sexy ass bike belonged to and he grimaced as he felt he was a bit out of his league with this one.

She pulled a thin knapsack from the pocket of her jacket, tucked the laptop inside and pulled two strings, before tucking her arms into either loop the strings made, wearing the sack like a backpack. She whispered, "See you at the compound." Jax hopped on the sleek black beauty, pulled her helmet on, and rolled away down the slight incline, not starting the bike up until she reached the bottom of the hill, careful to not wake any occupants in the neighborhood.

Walking to the door of his truck he muttered, "Well, fuck me."

8

I CAN HANDLE MYSELF

S he laughed out loud as she drove through town. Her activities of the night, seeing the look on Dodge's face as she climbed on her bike, and feeling the warm night air blowing across her face was all thrilling. She'd done what she set out to do. Nabbing the laptop was a bonus; she'd shown Dodge she was capable of doing a great job and by the look on his face, she'd done just that.

Now, to get the laptop to the compound and let Gaige work some magic on it.

At the thought of Gaige her stomach twisted. She'd no doubt be receiving an ass chewing when she got back for ditching Dodge. Hopefully the fact that the mission was a success, or maybe it was, he'd get over his piss-offed-ness, if that was a word, sooner rather than later. The last time she'd made him angry he didn't talk to her for a week.

All that aside, she completely understood that this was a serious situation. What they'd just come upon tonight was quite possibly criminals planning something more than likely illegal. Possibly deadly. Maybe both. She hoped more than anything that the laptop held some information that would be helpful. If not about tonight's activities, at least where "down there" was and hopefully, if Gaige would allow it, she could head to wherever that was and see what was going on. She vowed to herself that she could work with Dodge. He seemed to soften to her while they were on recon tonight and he might be useful in his big Tarzan kind of way. Since there was no danger of any kind of entanglement between them, it should be no problem. At least if she told Gaige all of this he might soften to her insubordination earlier tonight.

Pulling into the garage, she set her helmet on the mirror and inhaled a deep breath before hitting the elevator button. No doubt Gaige was watching her right now, so she didn't want to show fear. The doors closed her into the metal cubical and the slow ascent gave her a private moment to steel herself for what was to come. She whispered to herself, "Be contrite and sorry."

The doors opened and she jumped when Gaige stood before her, arms crossed over his massive chest, legs spread wide, jaw tight. Shit.

Locking eyes, she waited a beat without saying anything. When the doors began closing she reached out and stopped them, then stepped into the hall. Gaige didn't move which meant they were now standing quite close to each other. So close she could smell the spicy scent of his aftershave and if her hearing was accurate, he just ground his teeth together. This was bad.

"Gaige, I'm sorry. I was mad." He stepped back, but only slightly and she continued. "He messed up my mission last night and I didn't want to work with him."

Finally he responded. "I'm team lead. Not you. Me.

When I partner you up, you listen. That's one of the first rules of this whole group. We don't survive if someone goes rogue. We don't survive if agents begin deciding to act without the group in mind. Do you understand me?"

"Yes." It came out as a whisper.

"Say again."

She straightened her shoulders, cleared her throat and loudly responded. "Yes, I understand. I'm also very sorry."

His nod was slight, almost imperceptible but it was there. So, she continued in hopes that she brought good news. "We got a laptop from the house."

Tugging on the strings of the knapsack, she pulled it from her shoulders, pulled the laptop free from inside and handed it to him. "Also, there's a meeting happening next week. The only thing we heard was, 'I'll see you down there next week.'" Tucking a wayward strand of hair behind her ear her excitement bubbled up. "I'm hoping wherever that is it's on that laptop."

Gaige turned with the laptop without saying anything more. So it would be the silent treatment for a while. She'd deal. He entered the computer lab and a buzzer sounded on the intercom. He pushed the button, "Yeah."

"It's Dodge." The familiar voice sounded and a little chill ran through her body. She moved her shoulders back and forth to dispel the feeling and quickly walked to the elevator and tapped the override button. Waiting for the elevator to descend she smoothed her hair back into its ponytail and swiped under her eyes with the pads of her forefingers.

The doors slid open and her breath caught in her lungs. For the first time she noticed that his hair was blond with the ends lighter than the base. Must spend a fair amount of time in the sun. And had she ever seen eyes so green? Almost catlike. He exited the elevator and walked to the computer lab door without a word, but she noticed that his brows furrowed and his full lips frowned. Opening the door, he stood back allowing her to enter the room before him. His masculine scent was part musk and part something akin to Old Spice. Her dad always wore Old Spice. It was one of her favorite smells to this day.

"Dodge, welcome back. Just taking a look at the laptop Jax brought back. What are your thoughts of the evening? Let's debrief."

Gaige pointed to a chair next to his and she watched as he gracefully sat, surprised that a man his size didn't flop down and grunt. She pulled another chair up from the conference table and tried not to be irritated that Gaige was all but ignoring her.

"We witnessed four parties leaving the house besides Mangus, one at a time. Nothing of note. Their various modes of transportation are an '06 Ford Fusion. Silver, nothing special. A newer, possibly a '13 Dodge Avenger black in color. A '12 or '13 Ford Focus. White, an older, possibly 2000 or so Buick Regal. Deep red or burgundy - that's the car Mangus left in alone. All of them have Indiana plates. All the men looked younger, maybe in their early twenties. My guess is this is a recruiting ground for Mangus. Invite the young ones over. Tell them how excited he is to be working with them, tell them how important of a role this is, and then they'll give them the jobs that are the most dangerous. Likely loading or transporting product because they'll be expendable. Since Victor's men have scattered, they're likely trying to refill the void."

Gobsmacked. She couldn't believe he'd gathered all of

that information in the time they were there. It was difficult not to be impressed.

"Great intel. I gave Ford log on information for you to access our systems. Please type this into your report when you get home. I'll tell the others and we'll be on the lookout for those cars. I'm guessing the fact that they met somewhere in town and not on the Ryker Mountain that your assumption is correct. Mangus is keeping the newbies ignorant of any information that could get him caught."

Dodge nodded slightly, looked at her and their eyes locked. He nodded at her once then stood. "I'll let myself out. Do one of you need to get me into the elevator?"

Gaige interrupted her admiration of Dodge, "Jax, help Dodge get out of the house. I have his pass for the elevator and the code to get into the house on the desk upstairs in the office. Make sure he gets that information on his way out." He finally turned away from the computer he was working on, "Dodge, welcome aboard and great job tonight. Sorry it started out rough, but that won't happen again." He rubbed his chin then said, "You guys need to be here at 8:00 a.m. to meet the others."

Figures, he had to say it. Without looking at her Gaige turned back to the laptop, plugged it into the unscrambling device to access the password as she walked to the door. Dodge quickly stepped around her and opened the door for her. Once they were in the hall, she waived her access card in front of the elevator then looked into his eyes. "You don't have to open the doors for me, Dodge. Around here, I'm one of the guys."

"I wasn't raised that way. Can't change forty-something years of training, Jax."

She shrugged and found it hard to look away from

him. "Just sayin' you'll get teased from the others if you keep showing me deference."

The elevator doors opened and he waited for her to step in. She stifled a chuckle as he responded. "I can handle myself."

9

THIS WAS A 'THING'

S o, they were in. This was a 'thing'. Well, if he were being honest, the operation was spectacular. What he'd seen of the technology was extraordinary, too. There was quite a thrill to be making the kind of money they'd thrown about at their first meeting. He'd be banking a cool million in no time and there was more where that came from. The bonus was he'd be doing work he loved, with his friends, and the business of who's not paying, finding the work, and the like, wouldn't fall to them. Something Ford had been complaining about more and more lately.

Snagging his truck keys off the table he headed out the door. His house was newly built like Lincoln's house, but he didn't have a sister who was an interior decorator to help him out. Josie, Lincoln's sister, had offered to assist him too, then she'd gotten a big hotel job and that had taken all of her time. He had to finish the house on his own; it wasn't bad, but it wasn't the way he wanted it to be. Since he spent every spare dime saving to pay off his mom and dad's house for their anniversary, money wasn't there just yet for him to decorate his house. So, a few pictures had been hung, older furniture and white walls were what he had. And he didn't mind it, until last night. Walking into the mansion or what did they call it? The Compound. Seeing the little touches with the statues, colors of the walls, and the expensive furniture made him realize he needed to finish his house so he had that same feeling when he walked into it. After a couple big paychecks, he'd do that. It had been his dream for years to pay off his mom and dad's house for them and that was priority one. It was the least he could do for all they'd done for him. And if he were honest, he'd been a shit when he was growing up and living at home. Then there was the fallout when Adam died. He'd been depressed and in a bad state of mind and they'd been there. When he found out his wife was responsible for the accident that had killed Adam, he was inconsolable. They'd been with him through it all. So in his mind, this was a payback of sorts for all he'd put them through.

Inhaling deeply, he smiled and let the fresh clean air on this side of the mountain and the river cleanse him. Every time he thought about Adam his heart broke just a little bit more. Time did heal wounds, even deep ones, but not his. At least, not completely, probably never. You couldn't lose a child and not feel it deep inside - forever.

Shaking his head, he brought his thoughts back to the present and his peaceful place on the mountain. He was somewhat secluded over here, just across the river from Lincoln and Skye and at the bottom of the mountain, lovingly named Lynyrd Station on the Hill, that Ford and Megan owned and lived on, a couple miles up above him. They were all close enough in proximity so they could meet up in a moment's notice if trouble was lurking and far enough away that they weren't in each other's business. It was perfect.

He took a good look around, hopped up into his truck, and chuckled as he did. Of course he had to drive a Ram, it would be sacrilegious not to. The deep charcoal color captured his attention the second he saw it and this baby was his. Love at first sight.

Turning the key, he smiled again when the engine growled to life. Sexy. He pulled out of the garage, hit the button on the headliner, and began his drive to the compound for the second meeting in as many days with his new team members.

Enjoying the drive, it was difficult to believe that yesterday he'd been in such a pissy mood. The saying is true - What a difference a day makes. Turning the knob to turn the radio up, Chris Stapleton crooned Tennessee Whiskey and he sang along as loud as he could. The sun made everything seem just a little bit better, life was looking good.

Pulling up to the drive of the compound, he pulled his card from his pocket and waved it before the electronic pad at the gate, the gorgeous black wrought iron gate silently slid open and he pulled in. He saw Ford's truck already there, but Lincoln's wasn't. Not unusual since he and Skye married; the lucky bastard was probably getting laid. Stepping up to the front door he entered the passcode he'd been given last night, smiled when it worked the first time, he didn't trust Jax not to fuck with him, then entered the house. The same feelings he had last night enveloped him. Opulence without being snooty is how he'd describe it.

"Dodge, come and join us, we're having a cup of coffee and shooting the shit til everyone gets here." Gaige called to him from outside the kitchen door. His Army boots, which he always wore, were soundless as he crossed the foyer and entered the kitchen. The aroma of freshly brewed coffee and muffins, or some amazing smelling baked delight, filled his nostrils and his stomach growled. Gaige laughed, "Same reaction from everyone else this morning. Grab a cup of coffee and a muffin and let me introduce you to the guys you didn't get to meet last night."

He quickly poured his coffee, he liked it black so no fuss. The muffins were in baskets on the counter each with little cards on the baskets stating the content. Apple, cinnamon and bran. Ick. He took a cinnamon muffin, set it on a plate, and made his way to the table where his new partners were seated.

Gaige began with introductions. "Axel Dunbar." He motioned to a man who stood across the table. He had broad shoulders, a bit shorter in height than him at around six feet two inches. His dark hair was long, badass looking but his hazel eyes were sharp and intelligent. Axel leaned across the table, hand extended, and a ready smile on his face. "Nice to meet you Dodge. I understand we missed the fireworks with Jax." He chuckled as he sat again and two other GHOST men at the table laughed as well.

"Wyatt Lawson," Another man introduced himself. Standing he reached over and shook Dodge's hand with a firm grip. "Don't worry about Jax. She's excellent at her work, but she has a Spanish temper that flares up and then cools down. She's passionate in everything she does. She'll come around."

A stone sat hard in Dodge's stomach at hearing the familiarity with which Wyatt seemed to know Jax. Briefly glancing at the man, he guessed women would think he was handsome with his jet black hair and amber colored eyes. The dimples in his cheeks could automatically get him laid, even with the scar that ran down the left side of his face, and he wondered if Wyatt and Jax were an item.

The third man at the table that he hadn't met yet added, "She chewed me out once for not washing my dishes." He stood with his large hand out to shake, "Hawk." The massive man at around six feet eight, green eyes that sparkled and were mesmerizing against his tanned skin and thick black hair, was a beast. "I don't like doing dishes." He finished, nodded to the chair next to Dodge, then sat in his own. Man of few words.

Looking across the table at Ford, his old friend smiled, said, "Morning." Then sipped his coffee.

Sitting in his chair Gaige began the preliminaries. "We don't talk business up here, this is social. When Lincoln arrives and Jax and Josh come down for breakfast, we'll head to the computer lab and discuss our plans for today. In the meantime, get to know each other. I'm going to check on progress on the unscrambling of the laptop, it's been running all night.

Gaige stood and left the room, refilling his cup on the way. He could be heard faintly in the foyer, "Good morning, Lincoln. They're all in the kitchen. Grab something to eat then come on down for mission briefing."

10

LEADER OF THE PACK

Waking to the sun streaming in through the tall windows in her bedroom, Jax sat up in her comfy bed and stretched. She pushed back the weighted comforter she'd initially resisted, but then grew to love because it helped reduce her anxiety. She'd had plenty of that since Jake was murdered. A quick glance at the clock showed her it was 7:30 a.m. They were to meet the bounty hunters again today and her curiosity about the laptop came to the forefront of her mind. Actually the laptop and Dodge came to the forefront of her mind. He hadn't said anything to Gaige last night about his irritation with her. His lightning quick assessment of the cars in the drive and opinion that this was a recruiting ground were two things she hadn't deduced from their recon last night. So, he was smart, trained, and it didn't hurt that he was handsome - if you liked that sort of man. Tall and brawny, sandy blond hair and green eyes. Probably most women liked his type. Although he'd shown her his true colors the other day when he'd assumed she couldn't handle herself, she was willing to give him a shot but not a big one - just in case he played Tarzan on her again.

Stepping out of bed, she gathered her clothes for the day from her dresser then walked softly to her private bathroom. One of the things she liked most about this house was that they each had their own space without the work involved in taking care of it. GHOST offered them room and board and maid service, too. Sometimes they took turns cooking but Kylie was their cook some days; her mother, Mrs. James, was their main cook and house-keeper. That suited her just fine because she hadn't inher-ited the domestic gene from their mother, who was more domestic than many. She cooked, cleaned, did the laun-dry, and generally, took care of all of her children and her husband with pride and determination. Jax had hated anything domestic growing up preferring to be outside beating up a boy who tried telling her she couldn't do something.

Letting the shower warmup, she undressed, tossed her bedclothes into the black hamper in her bathroom, and unbraided her hair. Finger combing her long dark tresses she smiled at her reflection in the mirror as the light caught the waves. She inherited from her mother her petite nose, oval face, narrow arched brows, and clear skin. Her mother had been angry at her when she'd gotten her first tattoo. A small heart with the infinity symbol through it and squiggles and dots alongside on the inside of her forearm. It was a comfort when she looked at it. A tribute to her father, she'd listened to his favorite song, Neil Diamond's Hello Again, Hello, while she got this tattoo as the tears streamed down her cheeks. It was the last time she'd cried. Even after Jake was killed, she hadn't cried, she'd gotten pissed off instead.

Looking at her tattoo, the fingers of her right hand smoothed over the taut skin and she could swear she heard Neil Diamond singing.

Shaking the melancholy from her mind, she stepped into the steaming water and let it engulf her. Washing her hair and body, she thought about what she had to do to get to Mangus. So the next thing was finding out where "down there "was. Maybe she'd have a chance at getting to him then. That man needed to go down. He had no redeeming qualities. The way he manhandled her the other day showed her he had no respect for women. And, until Dodge interrupted, she knew he'd have taken her home and tried to fuck her. That said volumes for what kind of a husband he was. And then there was the bullshit he was involved in that was illegal as fuck. So, better to wipe him off the face of the earth and ensure this group didn't grow its body count because of him.

Stepping from the shower, she snagged a fresh fluffy, white towel and wrapped it around her body, tucking the front into the edge. She dragged a brush through her hair and made quick work of braiding it for the day. Donning clean clothes, she made her bed, the only domestic thing she did thanks to her training in the Army, pulled on her black Army boots, and headed downstairs for breakfast.

Voices sounded from the kitchen and she took in a deep breath and let it out before entering. Day two for their new recruits. She hated getting to know new team members. It slowed work considerably and this mission, above all, meant everything to her. She wanted it done and over sooner rather than later. She'd give these bounty hunters two days to get their stupid pink diamond, then she'd just take care of Mangus. After all, she was a sharp-shooter. She'd happily lay in wait for him somewhere and pick him off getting in or out of his car. That would be easy to do.

"Jax, good morning." Josh called to her. A quick glance around the table told her they'd all bonded over coffee - what a bunch of women these men were.

"Morning. Looks like you ladies had a coffee klatch for hours here."

Hawk, who usually said little to nothing, snorted and his green eyes landed on hers. "Careful pigtail."

She grinned, then he did. She grabbed a coffee cup, a bran muffin and leaned against the counter looking at the table full of testosterone. "So, what's up today?"

"As soon as you finish, we'll go down to the lab and see what Gaige found out on the laptop, make some plans and execute them." Her brother offered.

She nodded, bit into her muffin, and sipped her coffee as the men continued with their discussion of trucks. More than once her eyes landed on Dodge and more than once she'd caught him looking at her. She'd be lying if she said she didn't have a physical reaction to him. Her tummy swirled a little every time their eyes met. In the morning light she could see the highlights in his hair and the outline of his muscles through his t-shirt. Impressive.

The absence of a wedding ring, nor a mark where one had been, meant he wasn't married, but that didn't mean he didn't have a bounty bunny or were there bounty bunnies around? Lord knew most of the men in this room saw their share of action, her brother included. She didn't know much about the bounty hunters. Women loved big men, big muscles, and big personalities. What did she love? Respect. That was easy.

Finishing her muffin, she set her plate in the sink, refilled her coffee cup, and left the room to head down to the computer lab. She giggled to herself when she heard the chairs slide away from the table and footsteps behind her. The song *Leader of the Pack* floated through her mind and she smiled.

DAMN RIGHT I AM

The instant she'd walked into the kitchen, his mind split in two. One half tried to concentrate on the conversation at the table about trucks and some of the cool gadgets these guys had in theirs to help them with their jobs. He and his buddies would be able to have their trucks outfitted for service as well. All they needed to do was to make an appointment with their mechanic. First thing tomorrow that's what he'd do, but he had to ask again for the name since Jax held the other half of his mind and he didn't hear that part. With hair freshly washed and pulled back into the braid she'd worn last night, she looked refreshed and ready to take on the day. He'd be lying if he said he hadn't thought about her hair, and how it looked when she sat across from Mangus, falling free from the braid and waves upon waves. Lord help him, even the way it looked as she'd sat on his chest glaring down at him outside of the Copper Cup. She was pissed for sure, but when he looked up at her the way the setting sun wove copper and gold through the dark strands imprinted itself on his brain for some stupid reason

Then his eyes repeatedly locked with hers as she stood at the counter, one foot crossed over the other, eating that gross bran muffin, drinking her coffee. Damn, it was almost unnerving. Her dark eyes shined in the morning light and the look in them was undecipherable. Was she sizing him up or was she trying to figure out how to best him? It bothered him that he couldn't read her.

When she finished her muffin, set her plate in the sink and left the room without a word, all the others stood and left behind her as if she was the alpha and they were all betas waiting for her move.

Stepping into the elevator he eased his shoulders back slowly to lessen the tension. Staring straight ahead he felt he could get his bearings and stop letting her confuse him. Then the doors closed and he found himself more uncomfortable than ever even with all of these giants in the elevator with them. It felt oddly as if he wasn't even in his body. Maybe they spiked his coffee.

The doors opened and they all walked across the hall to the computer lab. Gaige turned in his chair to address them. "Have a seat and I'll show you what I've found on the laptop Jax brought back."

Each man took a seat and he was relieved when Jax sat between Hawk and Josh. Positioning himself on the other side of Hawk meant he couldn't see Jax and there was no chance of their eyes locking. Perfect.

"Okay. So here's what I've got so far."

The projector screen slid down the wall and Gaige tapped a couple of keys bringing the laptop's desktop onto the screen. What they saw were three columns of folders, all alphabetized. Gaige moved the cursor on the screen and pointed to the last folder in the first column named Organization.

"This file contains a few things of interest." He clicked it open and several folders appeared again, all named with three initials. Clicking on the first one, named IOM, the contents were all documents and one spreadsheet, named with only a number - 1, 2, 3 and so on. Gaige clicked on 1 and a picture opened up of the red-haired man called Ian that he and Jax had seen at the house last night escorting each person outside.

"This is Ian O'Malley according to the file in this folder on him. Ian is also the deed holder of the house where Jax and Dodge saw a recruiting meeting going on last night." Gaige looked at each of them then continued. "Ian seems to be the source for bringing possible recruits to Mangus."

Gaige clicked open a spreadsheet with a list of names. Next to each name was a date, followed by either a yes or no.

"Each of these yeses has a file in this 'Organization' folder that is similar to Ian's. A picture and other information but no spreadsheet. So I'm assuming this is Ian's tracking of the recruits he brings to Mangus. The dates are the meeting dates and the yes or no means he's hired or not. The names next to the noes don't have a file, but I have a hunch and I'd like two of you to check it out. That being, what happens to these men once they've met Mangus but are not accepted for the job since they know about him. We might be able to find one or two of the six on this list and see if we can get any information from them."

Axel responded quickly, "I'm in." He then looked down

the table, his hazel eyes were sharp and framed by his longer dark hair. He had a scar down the right side of his face, he looked menacing, but upstairs he'd seemed anything but. "Lincoln, you want in on this one?"

Lincoln smiled, "Absolutely."

Gaige finished, "Good. I'll send all information in this folder to your phones." He went back to the desktop with the three columns of folders and clicked on one named "Mags."

"Mags it appears is a partner, though minor partner, with Mangus. She lives in a town called Kingsdale, Arkansas, deep in the Ozarks. She owns a small cafe in a town of about 120 people. But yet, she can afford this." He opened a picture and a gorgeous brick southern planta-tion style house appeared on the screen completely adorned with a wrap-around porch. Flower baskets hung from the roof of the porch while each railing held baskets of brightly colored flowers. It sat high on a hill on what looked to be four or five acres neatly finished by an eight-foot-tall wrought iron fence. Every eight feet had a wide wrought iron post with a majestic horse welded between them. Imposing wasn't a strong enough word. "According to the information in this file, Mags and Mangus have been working together for many years and met when he was there looking for a place to do business."

One of the men around the table whistled as they all stared at the large mansion before them. "So tell me how in a town of 120 people she earns enough money in her cafe to support this massive house? That's the next mission. Find out what exactly Mags does for Mangus and how much of it she does. Dodge, I'd like you and Jax on this as I think this is the 'down there' they were talking about last night. I'd also like Josh, Ford and Wyatt on this one."

"Yes." He responded as the rest of the mentioned members responded in kind. His eyes sought Ford's and the smile on his partner's face said it all. Ford was eager to go on a real mission once again. How Megan would feel about that would be a different story. But that exchange surged through him and he felt his excitement grow, too.

"Good. Hawk, I need you here to help me out with the next little discovery this laptop uncovered for us. It appears that the outcropping you found on your recon yesterday holds the entrance to Mangus' hideaway. Are you in with me on this one?"

"I am." Hawk responded and said nothing more. Dodge looked around the table at the group he was privileged to be amongst and his heart beat a bit faster. He was back in it. For the first time since his military days, he felt excitement at doing something that held a bit of intrigue, a bit of danger, and a whole lot of benefit if they succeeded.

"Okay, you all get packed and ready to leave." He glanced at the five of them heading to the Ozarks. "The rest of you give me a few minutes to send you the information you need. Make sure you're all connected to our systems and bounty hunters?" He waited until they responded. "We have a rule here, you check in every three hours. Your teammates will help you out with that."

Dodge nodded and stood, eager to get outside and suck in some fresh air before his exhilaration got the better of him. As he reached the door to leave, Jax approached quietly and his manners kicked in as he opened the door for her. Hearing chuckles behind him,

Wyatt ribbed him, "Awww, look guys, Dodge is being a gentleman."

Waiting for Jax to exit the room in front of him, Dodge stood back and held the door open wider for Ford, then Wyatt to exit. "Damn right, I am." He said with pride. The ball breaking would now begin. In the Army that meant you were accepted. He'd take it.

12

THIS SHIT WAS GOING TO HAVE TO STOP

Okay, so she'd have a crew with her which would definitely hamper her ability to kill Mangus, but it wasn't impossible. Probably better that she kill him in Arkansas rather than here in Indiana, as that wouldn't draw undue attention to GHOST.

Pulling her duffel bag from the bottom of her closet, she dropped it on the bed, moved to her dresser, and began pulling out undergarments and socks from the top drawer. They seldom knew how long they'd be gone on a mission, but she was good at packing and bringing enough to get her through. She'd wash her undergarments out at night, usually Josh's too, since as the only woman she shared a room with him to save costs out on the road. That and making her bed, were the end of her domesticity. Washing her undergarments was a necessity. No matter how tomboyish she might be, she hated feeling gross. She only washed Josh's because he was her support system and it seemed like the least she could do for her only surviving brother.

That thought laid heavy in her heart and she renewed her resolve that a Santarino would pay for Jake's death. Victor was killed by Lincoln's wife, Skye, but he deserved that for kidnapping her. Jax intended to make sure his sibling paid the price her sibling had paid. End of discussion there. Those bounty hunters better find their diamond and fast.

Gathering three pairs of jeans and a handful of t-shirts she rolled them up and tucked them into her duffel. Entering her bathroom and pulling three laundry packs from the cupboard she tossed them into her duffel too. Mrs. James had pulled those together for her. Actually all of the team members had them. They consisted of a laundry pod, and a fabric softener sheet tucked into a Ziploc bag.

On her way out, she'd grab a few of the coffee packs Mrs. James made for them too. Those consisted of a k-cup, and for those of the group who liked creamer, there were creamer packs and sugar packs for those team members who liked their coffee grossly sweet and a coffee filter folded into each pack. She'd never been a sugar and spice gal, so black coffee for her was just fine. She'd learned to like it that way in the Army. It served her well in her life in GHOST as they traveled a fair amount and finding the perfect cup of coffee was often non-existent. The k-cups could be opened up and dumped into hot water and filtered out if need be. It worked if you needed it to work and sometimes they were out in the woods or sleeping in tents or their vehicles.

Grabbing her shampoo, conditioner and shower gel, she tucked them in the inside pocket of her duffel and zipped it up tight. Slinging her duffel over her shoulder she made her way down the massive staircase to the foyer.

Looking down on the house from the top of the staircase she admired the atmosphere and setup. The office was mainly Gaige's, though he did little work there. Only when he took calls from prospective clients did he hole up in there ironing out the gritty details of any given mission. Otherwise, he preferred being in the computer lab where everyone milled around when not on a mission.

The formal living room which no one ever used. Why they'd installed white carpeting in there was anyone's guess. Since they all usually wore boots and those boots mucked through some sloppy places they had no business schlepping across white carpeting, but good grief, there it was. The final door visible from the top of the stairs was the entry door, which was gorgeous carved wood and black wrought iron handles. It was also painted white but you could tell it was an artist's masterpiece at one time, the carving depicting horses in battle and soldiers engaged in the War of 1812 by looking at their uniforms. Most of this house was decorated with the military in mind, as the statues and figurines throughout the house held bits of American history.

She stepped off the last step and dropped her duffel next to the office door as they all did before leaving. She was the first one ready - as usual. Turning to make her last stop the kitchen she decided she'd have one last cup of coffee before leaving. Quickly nabbing four of her coffee packs, she filled a disposable cup with coffee and pushed the lid on securely. Walking to the back window she looked out on the grounds which offered her peace. She and Josh had planted a tree just off the kitchen window in Jake and their father's memory and she looked out on it now. The buds were beginning to pop open and soon it would be beautiful. Her right hand absently lay over the tattoo on her left forearm and her heart beat out a sad staccato. Whispering, "Miss you guys.", she inhaled and turned to see Josh standing at the kitchen door watching her.

"It's going to be a beauty when it blooms."

"Yeah."

"I see you're first again, so you don't have to buy lunch."

She smiled. They had an inside bet among the team members. Last one ready for a mission had to buy the next meal for all of them. "Hope those bounty hunters bring their wallets."

Josh burst out laughing. "We may have to exempt them since I doubt anyone told them about the inside bet."

"Bullshit. They'll have to learn somethings the hard way."

She watched her handsome brother, tall and lean, shining black hair like Jake's and their father, much like her own, walk to the cabinet and pull out his coffee packs. Tucking them into the front of his duffel, he turned and smiled at her. "I'm ready."

The front door opened and Dodge and Ford entered the house. Josh looked at her, "They won't be buying lunch. That leaves Wyatt."

They both chuckled and hers nearly died in her throat when Dodge entered the kitchen. He looked different. Battle ready and the look in his eyes was energizing and captivating. He was a warrior. Eager for battle. Ready to fight and win. The green of his eyes sharpened and the sandy blond hair even looked battle ready. His firm jaw, thick-corded neck and the stretch of his gray t-shirt across his impressive chest showed how firm and strong he was.

Josh broke the awkward silence. "You guys just made it in time. Wyatt will have to buy lunch."

"What's that all about?" Ford asked. Was it her or was Dodge staring at her?

"Last one ready for a mission buys the next meal." Josh moved to the side and opened the coffee cupboard. "Here's where you can grab your coffee packs for travel." He explained the coffee packs and Dodge finally turned to listen to him.

Taking that moment to breathe. Then swallow. She took a sip of her coffee and was irritated to find her hand slightly shaking. This shit was going to have to stop.

13

HITTING THE ROAD

Wyatt descended the steps just as the rest of them left the kitchen. "Son of a bitch, I have to buy?"

Josh laughed, "Yep, it's all you and I'm starving."

"Asshole."

"Slowpoke."

"Fuck." He turned down the hallway and headed to the elevator.

The rest of them grabbed their duffels and followed Wyatt. Jax stepped into the elevator behind Wyatt and Josh, Ford was next and son of a bitch, didn't he stand to the side and next to Wyatt. That left him standing right next to Jax. But at least standing next to her he didn't have to look into her eyes. She looked different somehow just now. Like a warrior princess, proud, strong, and ready to fight. It made his dick twitch in his pants and he sure as hell didn't need that kind of distraction. Besides, he didn't really even like her. She was a hothead and acted without thought. So, he'd try to partner up with Ford as much as he could, or Wyatt or Josh and he'd be just fine.

His energy was high right now. A thrill coursed through his veins at the thought of finding that pink diamond and bringing the company the money it would offer them. It was heady. But, there was a bit of a nagging feeling that he also kind of wanted Mangus to go down. This asshole was of the epic kind and he wouldn't stop no matter what. Even burying his brother did nothing to curb the criminal activity, just as if it was all in a day's work.

The elevator doors opened and he took in a deep breath to ease the vitality surrounding him. They all had that electricity around them and he wondered if they had an energy reading right now of what they would look like. Probably large rays of red and orange light. In their Army days, this feeling encompassed each of them before leaving base on a mission. There was something about the process of getting ready, packing, grabbing your gear, and knowing that you were about to face the enemy and it could be deadly.

Entering the computer lab one at a time they stood around the conference table as Gaige turned from his bank of computer screens and stood.

"You've each been sent the information we have on the location in the Ozarks, Mags Crowe, her real estate holdings, her business, and the town in general. Read up on it while you travel. I have new ear buds on the table for you if you prefer to listen to the information. Discuss your approach while you travel, I have the Beast ready for you. Josh, you driving?"

"Yeah, I'll drive."

"Okay, the Beast is programmed to get you to Kingsdale. I estimate it to take around six and a half hours or so. You should be there by dinner time or a bit later. Once you check into a hotel, call in and let me know the game plan. I'm tracking you, too."

"Okay." Josh responded, turning to the rest of them he locked eyes with Dodge first. "Let's go meet the Beast. You're gonna love her."

All he could do was nod. He sure as hell hoped the Beast was a big ass vehicle. Comfortable too if they were going to be sitting in her for over six hours. Just before leaving the room Gaige called to them once again.

"Dodge and Ford, leave your truck keys and we'll get your vehicles in the garage."

Fishing into their front pockets, they both grabbed their keys and tossed them to Gaige one at a time. "We'll take care of them."

They each loaded into the elevator once more and went down to the lower garage he'd heard so much about. As soon as the doors opened the light popped on and what met his eyes met was jaw dropping.

Wyatt stepped out first and began explaining the garage spaces.

"We each get two spaces down here for vehicles or whatever. These are my spots right here." He pointed to a big Ram truck in copper and rugged off-road tires with black accents. Next to the pickup lay a sexy sleek black corvette.

"Those are Josh's vehicles next to mine."

Josh drove a brand new Ford F-150 with all the bells and whistles. It was red in color and stood tall and proud. Next to Josh's truck was a matching red Mustang. Wow.

"These are Jax's vehicles." There stood a black Jeep with rugged tires and sexy rims and the black bike he'd admired last night stood next to it.

"Hawk's, Axel's, and Gaige's along this wall." Each

vehicle admirable in its own right and the garage bespoke of money and care. Every vehicle was clean and shiny, brand new and he felt like he was in a dream, if that dream included a sexy ass garage filled with exciting vehicles. That was a loud, affirmative. They'd made the right decision partnering up with this group. You could tell a lot about a person by how they took care of their vehicles.

"You'll all have those spaces at that end of the garage when you're here. This also serves as a bomb shelter and offers us maximum security should the worst happen and the enemy comes calling on us. Though it's doubtful."

Josh stepped forward and proudly waved his hand at the far end of the garage and toward a gargantuan black SUV with off-road tires, heavy suspension, and four doors. The bar over the top held a row of lights. He couldn't help it, "Wow, that is a beast."

Josh chuckled. "You haven't even seen the set up on the inside. Let's load up."

Josh tapped the remote in his hand and the lift gate opened. He tossed his duffle in the back then hopped in the driver's seat. Wyatt and Jax followed behind, stowing their gear so he and Ford did the same. Wyatt turned to Ford, "Why don't you sit in the front and begin playing with the computer on board so you get used to it. Dodge can do the same next stop and we'll have you trained on it in no time."

Jax climbed into the backseat of the Beast, Wyatt followed her in and Dodge saw her scoot to the middle. That meant for the next few hours, he'd be rubbing arms with Jax. He hopped up into the backseat, and smiled as his long legs had plenty of room for a lengthy ride. His smile caught Wyatt's attention. "I see you appreciate the room. I'm 6'7" and Hawk is 6'8" so when the Beast was built, we had the frame stretched so we could sit comfortably on long trips. Best thing we ever did."

Dodge's chuckle was infectious. Looking over Jax's head at Wyatt, he saw that his scar ran the length of his left cheek, curved down the back of his neck, and disappeared into his t-shirt. His longer dark hair mostly covered it unless he was looking the opposite way as he was now. When he turned his head, he caught Dodge looking at him. His smile grew broad, "Mission in the rain forest five years ago. Had a fight with a mad knife wielding suspect hopped up on PCPs and it was a fight to get him subdued. I owe Axel thanks for stopping him and saving my life."

Dodge nodded. "Glad Axel was there for you, man."

"So where'd you serve?" Wyatt asked.

"One tour in Bosnia, one tour in Indonesia for humanitarian relief after the hurricane. Then twenty years on the police force first as a cop then a detective for the last five." He responded, though for some reason it didn't bother him as much as it usually did. Probably because every person in this vehicle was former military. "Army."

Jax nodded. "Josh and I are Army, so was Jake and our father. I did a tour in Iraq beginning in 2002, then came home and joined GHOST. I've been here for close to fourteen years."

"Respect."

Jax giggled and it was the first time he heard her sound happy. It sounded good. Ford started sharing his story then. "I served in Desert Storm, came home, and married. Had a son, divorced his mother. Married again last year and now I have one son in Afghanistan and a baby girl at home. Battles of a different kind I guess. I've been bounty hunting for the past twenty years."

As they rolled down the road, Ford put the speaker on

in the SUV and they all listened to the information Gaige had pulled together. A plan formed in Dodge's head on what he'd do, but he'd sit back and see what the team did together and how they worked it all out. His stomach growled loudly and they all began laughing when Josh said, "Pull your wallet out, Wyatt, we're hungry."

14

THEY DIDN'T EVEN LIKE EACH OTHER

Okay, he seemed decent enough. They listened to Gaige's information and every once in a while, he'd nod his head. She wanted so badly to ask him what he thought about the intel. It would be good to get into their heads and see how they worked things. They being the bounty hunters.

Josh pulled the Beast into a restaurant parking lot, they'd only been driving for an hour and they were heading Southwest so not too far from home but strange land just the same. Dodge hopped from the SUV and she turned and followed Wyatt out of his side. Fighting the urge to look back and see the expression on Dodge's face. There was no reason to think he'd be upset. Why would he? But what she did notice was that his warmth was gone. She'd begun to enjoy his arm brushing against hers and she liked the smell of his aftershave or cologne or whatever it was. He smelled manly, much like he had last night. At the thought of how he'd held her tightly to his chest, her nipples pebbled, and she shook her head to shake the thoughts loose. She didn't need to go there.

At the restaurant door Josh and Ford entered and Dodge stood at the door and waited. When she approached he grinned at her and she grinned back.

He looked up at Wyatt, "Say what you will, my mama raised a good boy."

Wyatt shook his head and elbowed Dodge lightly in the gut but said nothing else, they'd probably save that for later. She almost wished she could be a fly on the wall to see what, if anything, the new guys would say about her. It was stupid to think that a discussion wouldn't take place. She was the only woman in a man's world and there would no doubt be a discussion. Comments. Something.

Shaking those thoughts from her head she decided not to get paranoid and go with the flow. These guys were nothing more than the other guys she'd worked with for so long. Actually the only teammate she'd ever had sex with was Hawk. Damned man was sexy as fuck. But they both knew the next morning it was a mistake and they'd never repeated it again. That was more than four years ago now. But there were times when she was lonely and she wondered if they could be friends with benefits. She hadn't had an honest to goodness boyfriend since she was in the Army. But once her boyfriend got out of the military, they wrote emails back and forth a bit and then those came less frequently then not at all. Trouble was, she wasn't all that sad about it, either. She never pursued him to find out what happened. Last year, she found out through friends that he had gotten married and despite a little pang in her heart, she was happy for him. She did stalk his social media to see what his wife looked like. Again, a little pang in her heart when she saw the blond beauty he'd married and how they looked at each other. He'd never looked at her like that. But then, she hadn't looked at him as if he was the only man on earth, either. That says something, doesn't it?

They found a circular booth and slid in, she scooted in behind Josh and Wyatt scooted in next to her. That meant Ford and Dodge were across the table from her and she'd no doubt lock eyes with Dodge once or twice during lunch, but that didn't mean anything.

A waitress with a frown came around, set water glasses on the table, not bothering to place them in front of any of them, dropped some menus on the table and said, "I'll be back in a moment, folks."

Not far enough south to get that southern hospitality. Ford moved the glasses to each of them saying, "Megan would have a fit if she saw that."

Josh replied, "Megan's your wife?"

"Yes, and when I met her she was a waitress and a damned good one at that. Before she was a waitress, she was a nurse. She can't stand shitty service and she's a bit outspoken about it. "

Dodge laughed. "That's for damned sure. I've seen her chew out terrible wait staff more than once."

Both men chuckled again and Jax thought she'd like to meet Megan.

Josh leaned forward, forearms on the table. "So, we don't talk about our missions in public, but what I want to do is discuss your ideas when we get back on the road. We need to call in and report back in two hours and I want to be able to give Gaige some sort of a plan."

Everyone nodded and Jax took that opportunity to mull over the information they'd heard on the way here. In her mind, she wanted to storm Mags's restaurant and demand to see that piece of shit Santarino, but of course that would get them nowhere and they weren't even sure what Mags did for Mangus. Though they suspected she was the stopping point for the border entry and she probably held the jewels and stolen art for a while until the heat was off, then repackaged it and sent it on to Mangus. That's what they needed to find out because she needed to go down, too. If she was working for Mangus, she was part of the operation, it all needed to end. And then there were the bounty hunters and their pink diamond.

"Okay, what'll ya have?" Their weary waitress barked.

Each of them ordered and then the conversation once again turned to cars and trucks. Something she was used to but grew tired of just the same. She wasn't a girly girl, but she didn't want to talk non-stop about vehicles and certainly not about their latest conquests. Luckily they usually tried to wait until she was out of the room before discussing anything like that, but she'd heard plenty over time and it mostly made her sad. She'd been with men before. Not a ton, but a few. But, she didn't want to be a one-night-stand girl. She wasn't looking for a husband either, but, what the hell, she didn't really know what she wanted in that department. So, it was just better to ignore that part of her mind and move on to taking someone down or taking out some aggression on the gun range. Truth be told, she didn't have any female friends, though Mrs. James and Kylie were nice enough and she'd sit and chat with them when they were cooking. But, she was a tomboy and talking about nail color and shoes was not her thing. No ma'am.

"Jax?"

She started when she realized she was being spoken to. "What?"

Dodge grinned at her, then repeated what he'd just

asked her. "I asked you what year your Jeep and your bike are."

"Oh, sorry. 2017 is my Nightrod. The last year Harley made them. My Jeep is brand new this year. They're wicked aren't they?"

"They are. Nice job with them." Dodge took a drink of his water at that moment and she tamped down the idea that maybe he was a little interested in her. He couldn't be, they didn't even like each other.

15

NOT A WORD WAS SAID

"Okay, let me hear your thoughts on the intel and how to proceed." Josh asked from the driver's seat. They'd just gotten back on the highway and their bellies were full.

Jax offered her ideas first. "I think we need to rent a car when we get there and split up a bit. We'll be wired and miked so we can talk to each other. But we need to check out the restaurant and see what kind of operation it is. We need to stake out Mags's house and the surrounding areas. Wyatt's our sharpshooter and so am I. We can be up in the hills watching for activity, taking pictures, and video. Once we know what's going on at both places, we can decide how to proceed."

"Okay. Next?"

Ford added his thoughts. "I agree with Jax on some points. I'm a specialist in ferreting out where hiding places and lairs are. Dodge is great at asking the right questions. Being a detective for many years he's learned how to separate the bullshit from facts. I think Dodge and Jax go into the restaurant and act like a couple vacationing in the area. Observe what's going on in there and report back. In the meantime, the rest of us can be close by getting intel from them as they see it. Who's there? What's happening, etc. They can either text us or tell us through their microphones and we can deploy from there when we have something. I've done this kind of thing a hundred times before. That restaurant is key. My guess, Mags goes in everyday and she either has people come to her or she's in the back on the phone barking out orders. But there's a reason she has a restaurant in a little town that couldn't keep a bank open and she's making money at it. I'd say people come in, order a glass of tea, hand off information and leave."

Josh responded, "I agree with you, Ford." He turned off the highway onto a county road and continued on, though at a slower pace. "Wyatt or Dodge anything to add?"

Wyatt spoke up. "I agree with Ford's assessment of the situation and think the plan is solid."

His turn. "I like Ford's plan as well. Being from the south I can tell you I also think she's likely running a protection business which tells me there's drugs or guns in the area, too. Those smaller towns are notorious for criminal activity. They're off the radar largely, and overlooked."

"Sounds good. That's how we'll proceed then."

He saw Josh's eyes flick to the backseat in the rearview mirror and land on Jax's. She smiled, "I'm good bro."

Just hearing that made his stomach settle a little. Then the thought that he'd been worried about her reaction kind of pissed him off. The object of this whole mission was to be successful, not spare Jax's feelings. The fact that she handled them going with a plan that was not hers spoke volumes for the kind of team player she was. That was probably why he felt better. This was their first test as a team and he was competitive enough to want it to work out.

Ford twisted in his seat and looked at him. "For Adam."

Swallowing the large lump that instantly formed in his throat he nodded once. "For Adam." But the words came out more like a whisper. They'd said this before every bounty they went out to hunt and before any mission that seemed dangerous. His son, Adam. It got him every time.

He lay his head back against the seat and the SUV grew quiet. When he opened his eyes again, it was an hour later. Josh was the only person awake and as Dodge slowly rose up he noticed Jax's head lay against his shoulder. He looked down on her shiny dark hair. Her full eyelashes rested on her clear, olive cheeks and looked so soft, like feathers, he had to resist touching them. Her hair smelled like a spa, clean and fresh and relaxing. Her arms were crossed over her belly and her lips looked soft and were slightly parted. He stopped moving so he didn't wake her. He could sit in the same position for hours, that's what his years in the Army and then on the force taught him. Sometimes you had to sit still to stay concealed.

He looked up to see out the windshield and the landscape only to catch Josh looking at him in the mirror. His expression was unreadable, just like Jax's and that unnerved him. He settled for a brief nod, then turned his head and looked out his window. His thoughts were jumbled at the moment and he needed to clear his head. He probably should have found some little hottie before he left and had a little fun, like the waitress at the Copper Cup who always flirted with him. All this was with Jax was simply that he'd been celibate for a few weeks now, for no reason other than he'd been busy. Clearly that was starting to get to him. Having sex with Jax was off the board, you don't eat where you shit, so to speak. It would be impossible to work together if they let things go too far.

Maybe Ford's plan wasn't so great after all. Acting like they were a couple could lead them down a path from which they couldn't return.

Josh slowed the SUV and turned down another road, then pulled into a gas station. "I've got to piss." He said quietly.

Wyatt woke up and stretched. "Me, too." He replied and opened his door. That woke Ford and then Jax, who looked up at him and mumbled, "Sorry." Then sat up straight. She scooted out after Wyatt and walked toward the convenience store and disappeared inside.

"You okay?"

He looked up to see Ford looking back at him. "Yeah. Long ride."

Ford grinned before exiting the vehicle and walking toward the convenience store, too. That left Dodge sitting here in the Beast. He didn't have keys to the SUV so he didn't want to walk away from it and leave it unlocked and he didn't want to lock it in case Josh didn't have the keys. He got out and stretched while he waited for someone to come back.

Josh was the first to arrive back. "I'll move the Beast to a pump and fill it up. Go on and relieve yourself, Dodge."

Nodding, he walked into the store, a little stiffer than he was when they first embarked on their journey and a lot more confused about his situation and these feelings that keep flooding over him. He was like a fifteen-year-old girl for fuck's sake.

As he left the store, Ford stood on the sidewalk waiting for him. "You alright, man?"

He looked at his friend. Those dark eyes held concern. "Yeah. A lot of new things happening in a short amount of time, man. Just trying to get my bearings."

Ford nodded and they began walking to the Beast. "Mind if I take shotgun for a while? I'd like to mess with the computers and familiarize myself with them."

"Not at all."

The Beast was almost full, the crew stood outside, everyone waiting to get in until they were ready to leave. Say what you like, six hours is a long time to sit in any vehicle. They were all in their forties, at least all of the men except Josh. Jax and Josh, if he remembered correctly from their intros was 36 or so. Still, old enough to begin feeling some of these missions.

"All set." Josh called as he hung the gas nozzle back onto the pump. He pulled the receipt from the dispenser and hopped up into the SUV.

Dodge jumped into the front seat without looking back. Not a word was said.

16

YOU MIGHT BE SLEEPING IN THE SUV

So, she'd be playing the happy couple with Dodge. Well damn. She wasn't mad, Ford had a solid plan, it was just she...hell she didn't know what was nagging her.

And, what was that "For Adam" comment? Who was Adam? Neither of them explained and she didn't want to seem nosy and ask, but she wondered just the same.

Only an hour or so to go and she had to admit, sitting next to Ford was nice and all, but not as nice as sitting next to Dodge. He filled that space up differently and she'd enjoyed brushing arms with him.

The Beast's phone rang and Dodge answered it through the computer so they could all hear. "Hello."

Gaige answered. "Hi everyone, I've got Lincoln and Axel here with me and they've been able to track down two of the men that were noes on Ian O'Malley's list."

Lincoln spoke up first. "The first person we found was a scrawny little runt named, Boyd Gorey. Boyd got nervous real fast when we asked about his meeting with Mangus and what he'd be able to tell us. He's not over 5 feet, 4 inches tall and my guess is he isn't big enough to be on Mangus' team. He insisted he didn't know who we were talking about and damned near pissed his pants when Axel leaned down real close and told him we'd be following him around unless he talked."

Axel could be heard in the background chuckling. With that scar running down the right side of his face, he knew just how to form his lips to make himself look positively scary.

"Anyway," Axel continued. "What we were able to weasel out of the little runt is they are looking for men to run loads between various locations down south and back to Lynyrd Station. We believe you'll be finding some interesting things down there in the Ozarks."

Dodge spoke next. "Did he happen to say how often he'd be running back and forth?"

Lincoln answered his friend. "Weekly."

Dodge nodded and sat back in his seat. "What about the other guy?"

"Right, David Boyce." Lincoln responded. "David met with a fatal car accident last week. He was out of town on a deserted road and ran down into a gully. DOA."

Dodge sat forward again. "Was there anything suspicious about the accident?"

"A lot. Rory, a good friend and a detective with Lynard Station PD, is looking into it for us, but I thought you might have some better connections with some of your contacts. Anyone you can call who might be able to speed up the info flow from the state?"

Dodge ran his hand along his jaw. "Yeah. I'll give Bobby a call tonight. Send me what you have please."

"You got it."

Gaige spoke again. "You all are only about fifteen

minutes out now, so we'll sign off. Hawk and I are going back out first thing in the morning to check out the entrance area. We believe he found it, we just can't figure out how to open it. Lincoln and Axel have two more noes to find tomorrow so we'll all report our findings once we have something."

Josh spoke up, "Sounds good. Once we check into the hotel, we'll check in one last time for tonight. Talk to you later."

Dodge reached forward and disconnected the call. His cell phone chimed then and he opened his text and read. She couldn't see the words he was reading, only the glow from his phone. He turned in his seat and looked at Ford. "I think Jared should try hacking into the records on this. For some reason, there's a slowdown of information coming through. I wonder if Mangus hired someone at the state level to hide information or severely slow it down."

"I'll text him. He can get into anything."

Her curiosity was piqued. "Who's Jared?"

Ford responded as he texted. "He's a friend of ours from the Army. He's a conspiracy theorist and fantastic information gatherer. He's got a data base that would impress the FBI and he manages to get intel that we'd never dream he could get."

She looked into the rearview to see Josh looking back at her. He smiled, which he didn't do often. "I think this is going to be a great partnership."

Dodge turned to Josh. "You like under the radar intel?"

"I like money. We get money when we successfully finish our missions. We stay aboveboard as much as we can, but bottom line is... we get our missions done to our clients' satisfaction. We don't break laws to do it, but how we gather our information isn't on the table."

Wyatt laughed next to her and it was impossible not to giggle. She liked the money, too. It made her feel powerful and free. She was supporting herself, by doing something she loved. She wasn't cut out for anything else in the civilian world. There might come a day, but she was saving money in wads, and soon she'd have enough that she could live on her investment accounts forever. She'd found a great financial guy who managed her money and he knew her goals. To amass enough money that if she was injured and couldn't work ever again, she'd be set for life. She was almost there. This job promised to help her realize that goal. Their customer on this job was a man whose daughter had been killed by one of the Santarinos. It worked out well that he was a billionaire in France and was paying them handsomely for this job. Bonus that she also wanted to stop Mangus to avenge her brother. When Gaige had told their client that piece of information the deal was done. He loved that they had a personal stake in this game. And after expenses they'd all earn a bit over a million dollars. Double bonus.

Josh slowed the SUV and pulled into a hotel parking lot. "Wyatt, run in and see if they have three rooms."

"Yep." Wyatt jumped out and she looked at Josh in the mirror again her brows furrowed.

He looked away without a word. She always stayed with him when they were on the road. With five of them on this mission that would mean she'd have her own room, which she didn't like mostly because it isolated her from the guys. She didn't like the special treatment, and she didn't like that she'd be considered separate from them.

Ford's phone chimed and all he said was, "Jared's on it."

Dodge nodded in the front seat and she heard a bit of a chuckle from him.

Wyatt came back out to the SUV, "We're in."

He walked to the back and Josh pushed the button on the dashboard to open the hatch. She slid out of Wyatt's open door and Dodge stepped out of the vehicle at the same time. She bumped into him, mumbled, "Sorry." Then quickly stepped to the back of the SUV to get her bag. The four of them walked into the hotel while Josh pulled into the parking lot and parked. She hovered in the lobby while Wyatt checked in three rooms for them. Ford and Dodge stood a few steps away, both of them looking badass. They were such a contrast. Ford was dark. Coal black hair and eyes darker than hers and Josh's. They looked like they were bottomless holes. Dodge on the other hand had sandy blond hair, worn short and green eyes that looked like green grass in the summer. Both were tall and broad and anybody would be totally stupid to try and piss one of them off. As bounty hunters she bet they always got their bounties.

Josh walked in and bumped her on purpose with his hip. "We can sleep comfortable tonight, Jax. Stretch out and enjoy the rest, we don't know where we'll be sleeping tomorrow. I'll bunk with Wyatt and the bounty hunters can room together. We'll all have space to stretch out and relax, tomorrow is going to be a long day. Kingsdale is 45 miles away and it doesn't look like there's much there. Depending on what time we get done, we may be pulling into some fleabag motel if that town or one nearby has one. We can't come back here...policy, right?"

"Yeah. I just don't want to be treated differently. You know."

"I do. You're not. Enjoy it, tomorrow you might be sleeping in the SUV. I'll call in and let Gaige know we're here."

17

SEE YOU RIGHT HERE

Okay, a good night's sleep and they'd be on the mission. He felt good about it. Strong. Mangus was running. Hiding information, secret entry to his lair. Possibly killing people after he "interviewed" them and they didn't pan out. He'd been hiding since the feds shut Limitless down after Victor was killed and Limitless' illegal activities were finally ferreted out. But, now he was secretly recruiting, which he hadn't been before. At least not that they knew.

He waived the key card in front of their door lock and the green light flashed. Twisting the knob, he opened the door and entered their hotel room, Ford directly behind him.

Dropping his bag on the first bed he stretched as Ford walked past him and dropped his bag on the other bed.

"Was Megan pissed that you came on this mission?"

"No. She's probably happy to have the house to herself for a bit. Well, just her and Shelby. My sister will give her some relief if Shelby's colic flares up. Since we met it's been one thing after another and we'd both lived alone for years before then, so it's been an adjustment. A good one, but a little space is good now and then."

"Yeah. I get that. I'm going to change into shorts and take a jog. That'll give you time to call her without me hovering."

"Thanks, but you don't have to leave."

He chuckled. "Look, I like Megan, and of course you, but I'm not interested in hearing your phone sex."

Ford laughed. "Fucker."

Swiping his gym shorts from his bag he chuckled as he entered the bathroom. After taking a piss he changed into his black work out shorts and gray tank top. Exiting the bathroom he fished his socks and running shoes from the bottom of his bag, quickly pulled them on and tucked his room card into his arm band, along with his cell phone.

"See you in an hour."

Ford sat on his bed, his back to the headboard and pulled his phone up. Dodge smiled to himself, the man couldn't even wait a minute to call his wife. It was nice. Not something he'd ever really had or dreamed he would, but nice that his friends had found it.

After riding the elevator down to the lobby, he noticed the empty room was brightly lit, with nice brown leather furniture and large floral arrangements were placed here and there making it appear cozy even in its vastness. Only one clerk was behind the desk and it was only seven o'clock at night. Not a largely populated area they were in so hopefully that meant the hotel would be quiet.

Exiting the glass doors the sultry air hit him but it felt good. After riding all day, he needed this to get his brain working again and his body sated. He took off running, setting his pace steady and even. There were street lights for a good distance down the street so he took the lighted path and set his mind for a good long run. He'd sleep better tonight after he tired himself out.

Thoughts of Jax ran through his mind as he noticed a curvy woman entering a restaurant as he ran by. She was a puzzle. Gorgeous. Curvy. Strong and smart. She was a definite team player, which was not what he'd thought about her the other night. He'd love to know if she'd gotten her ass chewed after he left 'cause she sure deserved it, but he'd never ask. Gaige was responsible for his operation and it was his call.

His head needed to be on straight to work with her because his emotions about her were all over the board. One minute he thought she was a loose cannon and the next he thought she was capable. He had to stop his back and forth. Hopefully tomorrow would show him how capable she was and he'd have the confidence to finish this mission with her and be impressed in the long run.

Turning onto a side street, he entered a more residential area. Neatly trimmed lawns and picket fences met his eyes and the area's residents sat on their front porches or in lawn chairs in their yards as children played and neighbors talked. Everyone stopped talking as he ran by and probably discussed the stranger running down their street. He waved at a few people who called out hello to him but he worked to keep his pace even and didn't want to throw that by talking.

After four blocks he turned down another street and noticed the same neat and clean homes lining the streets. Another few minutes and he'd head back to the hotel.

A woman ran across the street a block ahead of him. Her long braid bounced on her back as she ran and his thoughts floated to Jax again. Shaking his head he blew out a breath, ran to that block, and turned his head to look down the street. On impulse he turned to follow her. His strides were longer and he found himself catching up to her. Slowing his pace just a bit his eyes landed on her perfectly formed ass. She was fit, firm, and strong as she navigated the streets, curbs, and landscape changes effectively. One block up and she turned the corner, but she twisted her neck and made eye contact with him and he saw her smile. Jax.

He quickened his pace until he was about four strides behind her and settled in while enjoying the view. They ran for another fifteen minutes and he was fascinated that she navigated the strange town expertly and without hesitation. Turning the final corner, she led them directly into the hotel parking lot. She slowed on the approach to the door then stopped and bent over, hands on her knees. Stopping alongside her he mirrored her actions and bent to catch his breath.

Huffing out a few words he managed. "You set a tough pace."

She giggled. "Actually, you set the pace." She breathed in and out a few more times. "I worked hard to stay a few feet ahead of you."

She turned to look at him and their eyes locked. Hers held a bit of humor in them and when she smiled it was like a punch in the gut.

"Inspiring." Was all he dared to say.

She stood and walked around in small circles, allowing her muscles time to stretch so she didn't cramp up. "I wasn't about to let you beat me, old man."

He laughed then. It came straight from his belly. "Little Mama, I could have beat you any time."

"Bullshit."

"We'll see next time. You up for an early morning run?"

"4:30?"

"See you right here."

She giggled and strode into the hotel and he smiled. He actually kind of liked her.

18

THE MISSION WAS ON

Rising at the butt crack of dawn and stretching to wake up she looked around the room. She'd tossed and turned all night and the reason was two doors down from her. Tall, broad, strong, and mind-bogglingly handsome.

Inhaling a deep breath and letting it out she pushed the covers back and stepped out of bed. Pulling her braid from the band she finger combed her hair and rubbed her scalp. Damn, that felt good. Making her way to the bathroom to take care of business she finished, washed her hands, and pulled on her jogging shorts and tank. She hadn't washed them out last night as she normally would have, but they'd have to do.

She filled a glass with water to hydrate and drank it down refilling it again and setting it on the dresser to drink as soon as she got her shoes on. She'd drink it down and then go down and stretch before they ran. At only 36 she was beginning to feel the signs of age, though they were subtle, but mornings were the worst. Her joints were stiff and her muscles took a bit of time to loosen up. She needed to stay ahead of Dodge this morning, so she had a bit of motivation to loosen up.

Shoes on, she drank her water, donned her arm band, slipped her phone, key card and a five-dollar bill into the back of it. She'd learned long ago to never be without a little bit of cash. Opening her door to step out into the hall she ran straight into the solid wall of a delicious smelling man.

"Whoa Little Mama, hang on." His rough hands grabbed her upper arms but it was too late, she was chest to chest with him. Well, not really since he was several inches taller than she was, they were more like chest to stomach. And, holy crap her body shivered and her nipples pebbled and her breathing shallowed. WTF?

"Sorry, what are you doing hanging outside my door?" Her voice cracked.

"I wasn't hanging out. I came to tell you we can't run this morning; we have to head to Kingsdale right away. We got word there's a shipment there right now. If we jump into the SUV now we may get there in time to intercept some activity."

He stepped back and she turned to see Josh walking toward them. His jaw was tight and her mind snapped to what this must look like. 4:30 a.m., her hair down, her body all tingly and tight and his hands on her arms. Gawd, it looked bad.

Dodge turned and saw Josh stop. He quickly said, "She's packing now, Ford and I will be ready in five minutes."

He walked past Josh and to his room. Smiling at Josh she turned and entered her room, closing the door behind her. It was none of her brother's business what she was doing especially since she wasn't doing anything inappropriate. And, even if she and Dodge did have sex, it wouldn't be his business or inappropriate. They were both single adults. Lord knew Josh had his fair share of one-nighters.

Quickly tossing her things into her bag she made short work of packing, she didn't want to be last. Flying into the hallway no one was there and she was met with a slight indecision, wait here or go to the lobby and wait. That was probably the safer bet, since if they'd already gone down she'd have to buy breakfast, so she walked the few steps to the elevator and jabbed the button.

The doors slid open and as she stepped in she heard Dodge call out, "Wait for us, Jax."

She hesitated only a moment before holding the doors open, needing to be a team player and all. That was the only reason.

The two men stepped into the elevator with her and she'd be lying if she said she wasn't hyper aware, she had to change the direction of her thoughts. This was dangerous.

They rode down in complete silence, which was nice. Still trying to wake up and feeling the sensations of moments ago, she didn't want to have to think. The elevator doors opened and she was relieved to see neither Josh nor Wyatt were down here. Since Josh had the keys to the Beast she walked to the water station alongside the front desk and filled her water bottle with the iced water in the container. When she turned around, Dodge was watching her. Then she remembered she was still wearing her smelly running clothes from last night. She grabbed her bag and said to Dodge, "I'm hitting the bathroom, I'll be right back. But for the record, I'm here, right?"

Dodge chuckled, "Yes, ma'am."

Tossing her bag over her shoulder she ducked into the women's restroom at the far corner of the lobby. The instant the door closed she rummaged through her bag and found her jeans and a clean t-shirt. Doing as Mrs. James had taught her, she rolled her shorts and tank and tucked them into the baggy with the fabric softener sheet in case she didn't get the chance to wash them out and so they wouldn't make the rest of her clothes smell. Picking her bag up she left the bathroom with a mental note to braid her hair when they stopped for breakfast.

Walking across the lobby she was just a couple of steps ahead of Wyatt and Josh as they exited the elevator. Smiling at them she teased, "Breakfast is going to be delicious." And continued out the door to the SUV.

The sun still hadn't risen in the sky but the pink glow from the east was on the horizon, it'd be a beautiful ride for a while. Wyatt stopped at the front desk to check them out and the rest of them walked to the Beast and tossed their bags into the back. Josh looked at Dodge and said, "Why don't you ride shotgun again this morning Dodge, you can learn how to work the messaging system while we drive." Josh's eyes then slid to hers briefly before he hopped into the SUV.

Heaving out a deep breath she jumped into the back, sliding to the middle and Ford jumped in next to her. Josh started the SUV and Wyatt was just a few moments behind them.

The second Wyatt was in the Beast he began. "So we have intel that a shipment entered Kingsdale this morning around 4:00. Our informant said two large white cube vans entered Kingsdale, stopped at Mags's cafe, and began unloading large wooden boxes of goods. Now if it were food supplies, the boxes wouldn't be wooden and they'd likely be labeled with the names of the product and the company on the side. These were mostly large flat boxes, which could hold paintings, and jewels or anything else meant only Mags."

Josh continued, "So the plan is, we'll get to just outside of town about twenty miles. There's a car rental place there, Gaige is getting someone to get in early to help us out, and Dodge will rent a car. He and Jax will go into the cafe for breakfast, look around. Use the restrooms and walk around outside as if you're having a cigarette. See what you can see. Mic up now. Dodge, the comms are in the console. Report to us on everything you see. We'll be close by, watching and waiting for word. Questions?"

Dodge opened the console and reached in pulling out neatly wrapped microphone units and handing them over to each of them. Their fingers brushed when he handed her unit to her and goose bumps formed on her arms. He looked her in the eye then and she found it hard to look away. The unspoken message was hard to define and she couldn't help but wonder if he felt the same bit of a thrill as she had.

She tucked her earpiece over her ear and ran the cord behind her and into the collar of her t-shirt. Wyatt reached forward, "Let me help Jax, and you can return the favor."

He expertly reached up under the back of her shirt and pulled the wire down and out the bottom. Tucking his into the back of his shirt, he leaned forward allowing her access to do the same. It was a routine that had been completed many times before. She turned to Ford and tapped him on the shoulder to lean forward. He followed along and she gently pulled the wire from under his shirt and handed it to him to plug into the receiver box. When she turned forward she caught Dodge looking back at her. Her heart beat a bit faster but wanting to act professional, she leaned forward and tapped his shoulder. He leaned up from the seat back and she reached into his t-shirt and her fingers skimmed along the warm skin of his back as she pulled the wire down. When she handed him the wire their fingers touched and he squeezed hers before releasing.

Closing her eyes she squeezed her thighs together to squelch the ache she felt there.

They tested their mics, but not the usual "test, test". Josh said into his, "I've never seen so damned many churches lined up on every street in every town we drive through."

Dodge chuckled, "They don't call this the Bible Belt for nothing."

After that, they each sat back and gathered their thoughts. Missions were no laughing matter and they all needed to be in top form. She usually tried to visualize their mission and completing it successfully to put her mind right and push doubt away. This was nothing compared to some of the missions she'd been on, but Dodge and Ford were new to their team and no matter that she knew they had been in situations like this before, they all needed to work together and they'd had so little time to perfect that.

Josh pulled into the lot of the rental agency and Dodge jumped out of the Beast. Josh pushed the button on the dash to lift the hatch and Dodge easily pulled his bag and hers from the back. She saw from the back of the truck that he entered the agency with both bags. She refused to look at Josh in the rearview, so she tapped Wyatt and he jumped out. When she jumped out behind him, he whispered, "Make sure you know what you're doing."

Their eyes met and she whispered, "Stay out of it." Before continuing on into the agency.

Dodge's back was to her when she entered and she drank in the sight. His black t-shirt showed the muscles of his back and that waist of his narrowed into the waistband of his jeans. From there, his fine ass and perfectly rounded cheeks practically made her fingers twitch with want of touching him. He turned and looked at her over his shoulder and those green eyes locked with hers and damn it, her heart raced as if she'd just been running. He grinned and signed the form the clerk slid across the counter to him, her eyes pouring over every inch of him. Jax had to grit her teeth to not go all alpha on that witch.

Dodge smiled at the clerk and she saw the woman, whose glasses made her eyes look larger than they were smile back at him and practically purr. Dodge bent over to pick up their bags and Jax decided enough of this crap; she grabbed her bag from Dodge's hand, slung it over her shoulder, and proceeded out the door ahead of him.

She heard him chuckle next to her and she chose to ignore him. "White Malibu in stall 105." He headed to the right and she switched direction and followed him. Tossing their bags into the trunk, the instant they were in the car her speaker beeped. "I'm here. Can you copy?"

Josh responded. "I copy. Dodge?"

He touched the ear piece, "Copy."

Josh continued. "Okay, head on down Highway 76 to Kingsdale. The town is so small there's no way to get lost. We'll stay about a mile behind you and when you turn into the town square, we'll keep going about a half mile out of town and wait for word from you."

"Roger." Dodge pulled from the parking lot and headed in the direction he was instructed to go. The mission was on.

19

MAGS

Watching the road as it turned into Kingsdale, he saw immediately there was indeed little there. The town square was nothing more than a regular residential block. In the middle was a small covered gazebo, which stood alone. On the right side were two business buildings, one a realty company, which was closed at 6:00 in the morning and next to it an empty looking building if the lack of signage or occupancy were accurate. A narrow road veered off of the left side of the realty company and the far side of the square, which held two more buildings. One a small store which boasted "Corks of all sizes "and "glass mason jars "painted on the window. A wooden bench sat out in front of the closed store and next to the store was another empty building. The left side of the square also held two buildings, one a bank and Mags's Cafe. The last section of the square held two more buildings, one a day care which looked as if it had seen better days and one a yoga place, which also seemed to have little to no business by the age of the signs in the window, which still advertised their "Easter

Special" even though it was July. These buildings, two each on each side of the square created a perfect square with the gazebo in the middle. Each business set itself apart either by paint color, siding choice, or shade of the shutters on each. But, all of the buildings were single story buildings and of similar size. Dodge pulled in front of Mags's Cafe, looked at Jax and said, "Ready?"

"Yep, let's do this."

He exited the car and walked around to the passenger side and opened the door for her. When she stepped out, her hair fell over her shoulders and the soft waves were nearly impossible not to touch. He reached forward for her hand and when their fingers touched, his heartbeat increased and his breathing shallowed. Then she looked up into his eyes and smiled and he thought he'd die right there. Her dark eyes sparkled and her smile was perfection. Her straight white teeth then scraped her bottom lip and he mumbled, "Well, fuck me."

She snorted lightly before whispering, "You wish." And he did. At that moment he wanted to toss her back into the car and take her somewhere private for the rest of the day. Instead he reminded himself of the mission and the money and put his head back on straight. He closed the car door, wrapped his arm around her shoulders, and when her arm snaked around his waist the thought ran through his mind that this may be the hardest mission he'd ever been on.

Opening the door of the cafe, the little bell over the door rang and Jax proceeded him inside. Three mismatched tables stood empty before the large front window. Three booths lined the middle of the cafe, with a half wall along the left side. Behind the booths was an old-fashioned counter with no stools. The door to what he presumed was the kitchen stood off to the right. He walked to the counter with Jax in tow, both pretending to look at the menu which was written in chalk on the board above the window that opened into the kitchen. A waitress walked from the kitchen, her curly, stringy hair in a messy array on her head was barely held back with a skinny headband. The aroma of fresh coffee filled the air and his stomach growled.

The waitress drawled, "How can I help ya'll?"

"Baby, what do you want?" He said sweetly to Jax. Her head tipped up and their eyes locked. She smiled at him and said, "I'm famished after last night. I'd like bacon, eggs and fried potatoes. Oh, and coffee."

He couldn't look away from her and he had to swallow three times to moisten his parched throat. Finally he felt he could speak without sounding like a teenager. "Make that two."

The waitress giggled. "You got it. Have a seat anywhere you like except the middle booth."

He turned them toward the front window but Jax halted and said to the waitress, "May I use the restroom?"

"Sure, hon. It's right on over there in the corner. Jiggle the toilet handle when you're done."

Jax looked up at him then and he couldn't help it, he leaned down and kissed her. The second his lips touched hers his heartbeat raced and his hands actually began shaking. He shouldn't have done it but he did. Too late now. He heard Jax whimper lightly and his tongue swiped out and licked her bottom lip. She let out a breath and he stood straight, slapped her ass and said, "Hurry back, hon."

Color him satisfied when he saw her freeze. He nudged her lightly and she shook her head then turned

stiffly and walked to the bathroom. Heading toward the
front window, he sat at the table to the far left so his back
was against the wall. He could easily see out the front
window, though there wasn't anything to see.

The waitress came to the table with two empty coffee
cups and a pot of coffee. She set the cups down, poured
the coffee without saying a word. Before she'd disappeared from sight a heavyset woman walked from the
back room and sat at the middle booth. She wore jersey
red shorts that dropped to her knees and an overly large
printed jersey shirt. Her thinning, dishwater blond hair
brushed her shoulders in an undiscernible style. Her
faded blue eyes landed on him and stared. Her age was
also hard to guess, but if he had too he'd say mid-forties.
He nodded at her and mumbled, "Morning." She merely
nodded once but said nothing. This had to be Mags.

Jax came from the bathroom and the first thing he
noticed was her cheeks were flushed and dammit that
looked good on her. He stood as she approached the table
and pulled out the chair to his left so she'd be looking
right at Mags. Once Jax sat, he slid her coffee cup to her
then locked hands with her, brushing a brief kiss over her
knuckles. Her cocoa colored eyes met his and he saw her
pupils dilate and her nostrils flare. Smiling what he hoped
was his most devastating smile, he leaned in close and
whispered, "Mags."

She looked at the table, acting the part of the shy
lover, and when he sat back, she picked up her coffee cup
and glanced at Mags.

A black pickup truck, covered in dust, pulled up to the
front of the cafe and parked next to their rental car. A tall,
thin man exited the truck and walked into the cafe with a
manila envelope, easily 9 inches by 11 inches or so, in his

hand. He stood before the booth where Mags sat, nodded at her and waited. Mags looked at him silently then nodded, and the man sat in the booth across from her. He slid the envelope across the table and whispered something to her. She responded to him and the only things he could pick up were "family" and "again".

He looked at Jax and she pulled a tube of lipstick from a small bag she had sitting on her lap. He hadn't even noticed that she'd pulled it from her duffle he'd been so engrossed in everything else about her. She swiped the clear gloss over her lips but left the tube on the table in front of her. Smiling sweetly at him, she took his hand in hers again and squeezed. "What should we do for the rest of the day, baby?" She asked and his mind went blank for a moment.

"I thought we'd do a bit of exploring. Isn't there supposed to be a horse ranch around here? Would you like to ride?"

"That sounds like fun."

The thin man stood and left the cafe. Taking a sip of his coffee he let his eyes shift to Mags and she pulled a wad of cash from the envelope, counted it in front of her, then tucked it into a zippered bank bag laying on the booth seat next to her. Her faded blue eyes veered to his and a small smirk lifted the left side of her lips, but her eyes never showed signs of humor.

Setting his coffee cup on the table he glanced at Jax, who had her phone laying on the table between them. He saw the microphone on the screen and assumed Josh was or all of the guys were listening in.

The waitress brought out their breakfast plates, refilled their coffees and he noticed that Jax smoothly lay her forearm over the screen of her phone so it wasn't visible to the waitress. Not that she seemed all that aware of anything around her.

Another man entered the cafe, and the routine was repeated. He stood at the edge of Mags's table waiting for permission, envelope in hand. As soon as he sat, the envelope was pushed across the table and low murmuring could be heard That's when Jax's eyes caught his and her smile widened. She moved her arm and he noticed the microphone pulsing as if it was catching voices. Slightly lifting her lip gloss to show him the small dot on the edge of it he realized it was must be a high-powered microphone and it was picking up Mags's discussions and relaying it to their team. They really did have cool toys.

Jax winked and his stomach flipped slightly. They ate slowly, and during their breakfast they witnessed four different men come and go. Mags seemed interested in them in between. Probably not used to seeing many tourists. At one point his eyes locked on hers and he decided to engage her in conversation.

"We can't help but notice there aren't any bars around here. Can you point us in the direction of the closest one?"

She folded her hands on the table top and exhaled before answering. "You're in the Bible Belt here, son. We can't serve alcohol within three hundred feet from a church and one thousand feet from a school in these parts. In case you haven't noticed, you can't throw a stone without hitting a church."

"Yes ma'am. We did notice the multitude of churches."

Never looking away from him, she pursed her lips as she seemed to select her words carefully. "Yes. So, I'm wondering what on earth two good-looking people like yourselves are doing in these parts. We don't have much to offer tourists in case you haven't noticed."

Jax smiled and took his hand. "We're just on a road trip. Our first one together to see if we can get along in a car for long periods of time. We don't have a destination in mind, just driving and stopping when the urge strikes. Unfortunately, after having a couple cups of coffee this morning, the urge struck just before we got here and I was so happy to see your lights on." Jax nodded to the restroom when she said 'urge' and Mags nodded slightly.

Mags pulled two sheets of paper from one of the envelopes on the table and spread them in front of her. Finally looking at her papers Dodge felt a bit of relief, but not fully. Mags watched everything around here and she was watching them, even if she didn't seem to be.

The waitress came around again and took their plates, quickly returning to refill their coffees once more and laying their bill on the table.

Dodge grabbed it, looked at the total, and then reached into his back pocket to pull his wallet out. Pulling a twenty from his wallet he dropped it on top of the bill and looked to see if he could catch the waitress. Mags said without looking up, "You'll need to take it up to the counter, you won't see that one again."

Dodge nodded and said to Jax loud enough for Mags to hear, "I'll use the restroom before we head out."

Jax smiled and to his surprise, she leaned in and kissed him on the lips. His cheeks heated, he could feel them burning and that was nothing compared to the heat that grew behind his zipper. He was actually afraid to stand right about then. Then, the little vixen purred, "Don't be too long, Tarzan."

Well, fuck him and a monkey, what was he supposed to do with that? He swallowed, inhaled once and exhaled before saying, "I thought my length was one of the things you liked best."

Her cheeks flamed a pretty bright pink and he enjoyed watching her chest heave as her breathing seemed to increase dramatically.

20

YOU HAVE THE COOLEST SHIT

She tried not to fidget in her chair but that just hit her right between the legs. The dampness and tingling down there made her positively uncomfortable now. She started it but, shit, she never dreamed he'd spike back that volley she lobbed.

Mags chuckled under her breath and Jax knew she was watching her. The woman was scary, she didn't miss anything. She acted like the nice southern woman, but Mags was running some scams here and she couldn't wait to get back in the car and find out what they'd captured on her microphone. Another truck pulled up outside and the routine was no doubt about to happen again. It was a great time to get outside while she was busy, that woman made her nervous. She was too watchful. Too calm for a woman running something under the radar in public. She sighed in relief when she heard the bathroom door open. Swiping her lipstick and phone she tucked them into her little clutch and walked to stand in front of the door. Dodge walked slowly toward her, glancing at the signs taped to the wall as he neared her. She felt jittery for some reason and she wanted to run from this place. Dodge saw her standing there and grinned and son-of-a-bitch, her nipples puckered. This just had to stop, this flirty thing they were doing.

He reached her finally and grabbed her hand. They exited the building and she breathed a sigh just to be out of there, the walls had felt as if they were closing in for some reason. Instead of taking her to the car, he pulled her to the little gazebo that stood in the town square.

"What are you doing?"

He stepped up into the gazebo, pulling her with him. Before she could grasp what he was about, he spun her around, wrapped his arm around her waist and pulled his phone up, taking a selfie with her. He snapped a few times then pulled her across the gazebo and took a few pictures of her by herself.

"Smile, Jax. We're on a road trip. New lovers and all."

The man who sat with Mags last exited the cafe and Dodge snapped a few more pictures with him in the background. Then it dawned on her what he was about. Smart.

They stood together in the gazebo and as the man backed up his truck Dodge pulled her into his arms and kissed her on the lips. Full on lip contact. Surprised, she froze, not sure what to do. Then his lips began moving over hers, teasing and softly caressing them. His tongue licked slowly across her bottom lip before his lips sealed over hers, their fullness so soft and sexy against hers. His tongue then slid into her mouth and danced with her tongue and any air she had in her lungs escaped. She felt like she was floating on a cloud, his strong arms wrapped around her, her body pulled tightly to his. A moan escaped from her throat and she heard it but then again it didn't register that it was her voice. His hand dove into her hair and grasped a handful of the glossy locks and she pulled her hips forward to rub herself on his thigh.

Every nerve ending was on fire. Her entire body was on fire.

He stopped kissing her lips and kissed along her jaw, over to her ear before swirling his tongue along the shell. Goose flesh erupted down her arms, across her back, down her belly and then it all pooled right. Between. Her. Legs.

She grabbed handfuls of his shirt to steady herself. Gulping in large quantities of air to get her bearings once again.

His head lifted slightly, as he stared into her eyes he slowly husked out, "Don't tease me again, Jax. I'm not a toy for you to play with. I'm a man, with needs and I happen to find you very sexy." To point out his comment further, he pulled her body tightly to his and she felt the steel rod he carried in his jeans and her knees shook.

Well, hell.

"You two often erupt into public displays of affection?"

Dodge straightened and took a step back. His arm wrapped around her shoulders, but he kept his front pointing at her side. Wouldn't do any good to show their visitor how much he'd erupted.

Dodge responded. "Once in a while. Is there an ordinance or something?"

The man who spoke to them was older than the dirt he stood on. His tanned, wrinkled skin sagged off his face. He wore bibbed overalls, a long sleeve flannel shirt, which wouldn't seem so out of place if the temperature wasn't already into the eighties and rising steadily. A brown cowboy hat was perched on his head, hands in his pockets and a grin on his face.

"Nope, no ordinance. We just don't see much of that in this town. We don't see much of anything here actually."

"We're sorry, Mister..." She hoped to get his name.

"Stan. No mister, just Stan'll do."

She smiled to put him at ease. "We're sorry, Stan. It's such a cute town square."

He chuckled. "I'd not push Mags too far if I were you. She runs things here and she'll give you a bit of leeway, but not too much."

Dodge leaned down and shook Stan's hand. "Mags doesn't like kissing?"

Stan smiled then and the few teeth he had left were a bit crooked. He leaned in and lowered his voice. "You see her? I'd say it's been years since that woman was kissed." He guffawed, purely entertained by himself.

Jax laughed she was so surprised by his comment. "We'll be moving on soon. We just wanted a couple of pictures." She stepped down from the gazebo and shook Stan's hand. "Mags sure seems to have a lot of male visitors for a woman who hasn't been kissed in a while."

Stan nodded, his lips thinned, then his tongue darted out to wet them. "That's all her bullshit business and extortion going on in there." Stan turned and walked to the closed store that sold corks and opened the door, disappearing inside.

Dodge stepped down and took her hand, leading her to the car. "Let's go, Little Mama."

Climbing inside the car, she waited until he pulled away from the gazebo and began driving out of town. Pulling up her phone, she tapped Josh's number, and then hit the speaker icon.

"You got some great stuff there. Are you gone now?"

"Yeah, where will we find you?"

"Just south of town about a half mile. We're at the loneliest gas station you ever laid eyes on. Keep driving past, we'll follow then pass you to lead to our destination."

"On our way." Ending the call she looked at Dodge's profile. Pulling out her lip gloss container she wiggled it in his sight. "Microphone, which attaches to my phone with one tap. Our designer calls it the iListen."

"You all do have the coolest shit."

21

FOREVER FOUR

He thought by kissing the hell out of her she'd back away and not be so damned cute. That didn't work. It seemed to do just the opposite. She was smiling like the cat who got the canary and chattering on about the town and Stan, wasn't breakfast so darned good and how much she loved missions. Every time he glanced over at her, her eyes sparkled, her smile was perfect, her giggling - well dammit, her giggling was adorable.

He past the gas station and Josh was right, it was lonely. A sad older neon sign flickered in the window and actually only said, "pe" the O and the N didn't go on at all. The Beast pulled out of the lot then passed them not more than a mile down the road. Dodge followed the Beast through some winding roads and wondered where they were going. Finally pulling out of town the road sign said they were entering Jasperville and it couldn't have been more different from Kingsdale. The buildings were plentiful and well kept. Cars and trucks were parked outside of the local stores and restaurants. Hell, there was even a hotel, though not a huge one, still it looked clean and decent.

That's where Josh led them, through the parking lot and to the back of the hotel. Parking at the edge of the lot near the grass, the three men exited the Beast each of them stretching.

"You caught some great stuff. As soon as Gaige has it all uploaded and secured, he'll send us the audios and you can listen to them yourself. Mags has a protection scam going on in town. Those men you were seeing come and go were bringing her the extortion money. Local farmers are paying to keep Mangus' men from stealing from them and killing them."

Jax responded. "Holy shit. It was obvious she was organizing something with each of those men. And the way they waited to be allowed to sit at her booth is positively weird. She's feared for certain."

Wyatt added his two cents. "The best part is for you guys," his eyes met Wyatt's. "We think she has the diamond. Or at least the jeweler who is getting ready to cut the diamond up into pieces."

"You heard that?" That was huge. He wanted that diamond back, it would be a boon to them, no doubt.

"Yep." Josh added. "Or at least that's what we think was said. Gaige is trying to magnify the audio now and see if he can clean it up. The word jeweler was said at the same time the waitress began talking to you so it was a bit muffled."

"Shit." The most important piece of information they got or a huge portion of it and that waitress had to come right then. She likely knew how important the information that particular man had for Mags and purposely came to their table then just to make sure they didn't hear anything. Not that she knew who they were. But, clearly strangers in that town were noticed and not trusted.

Ford finally spoke up. "We'll get it. We could clearly hear "pink" and "jeweler" but the other words were muffled. It certainly seems as though they at least know about the diamond, which confirms that Mangus is responsible for stealing it as we assumed. The puzzle pieces are coming together, Dodge."

He shook his head as he mulled over this information. "I saw two men unloading what looked like food stores from a truck parked outside the kitchen door, into the kitchen. But, since we were there for about an hour and no one but us ordered any food, I can't possibly imagine what they're using it for. When we left town the truck was gone, but if I see it, I'll recognize it."

Wyatt shook his head. "She's running a tight ship there and we also think we heard her order the murder of one of her minions. Though we aren't a hundred percent sure of that either."

"Holy fuck. That explains why I felt creeped out." He exclaimed.

Jax twisted and looked into his eyes. "You too? I couldn't wait to get out of there."

He chuckled. "Is that why you're waiting at the door for me?"

"Definitely. She's eerily quiet and watchful."

He laughed then and so did she. He looked over at the guys and Ford was grinning so was Wyatt but Josh looked like he was eating a sour lemon.

Jax changed the subject. "So why are we here and what's next?"

Josh responded. "We're going out to locate Mags's house and see if she has monitoring equipment and/or security and what that looks like. Why don't you follow us and we'll spread out once we find it? We're here because Kingsdale is small and everyone knows everything going on. A vehicle like the Beast is noticeable and likely already targeted. So, stopping to talk to you anywhere near that town is dangerous. Even here, though close to twenty miles away, is probably not safe for long. But we're here because we have one friendly in town that we know about."

Friendlies were local law enforcement that weren't on the take. Dodge felt disappointed in his police brethren who were, but assumed in a town like Kingsdale, it was likely a losing battle to fight against a group like the Santarinos, with strength and money.

"Okay." Jax turned to get back into the car but Josh asked, "If you want to ride in the Beast, Ford can ride with Dodge."

She smiled at her brother and shook her head. "I'm good. Ford, you okay in the SUV?"

"Yep, it's all good." Ford responded, that goofy grin still on his face.

Nodding at Josh, he and Jax quickly jumped in the car before Josh could say another word. He didn't want to have an issue with Josh. With any of the guys for that matter and he and Jax were finally finding some comfort level with each other, so it would be nice if that would continue. Going to work sucked if you didn't get along with your peers. Especially in the line of work they were in.

"He'll be okay; he just doesn't want me to get hurt."

"What?"

"Josh. He just doesn't want me to get hurt. He still

thinks you were leaving my room this morning and he's just being a protective brother."

"You didn't straighten him out on that?"

"I haven't had the time, Dodge. And, besides, it's none of his business who I sleep with."

"We didn't sleep together."

"Doesn't matter. It's none of his business. I don't make judgments on the women he sleeps with and believe me, there have been some doozies."

"Has he ever been married?"

She wrinkled her face, "Almost. She left him at the altar."

"That sucks."

"Yep. What about you. Have you even been married?"

He took a deep breath and let it out slowly. "Yeah. I was married for eight years."

She visibly swallowed a lump in her throat and he wondered if that bothered her. Then she continued, "Do you have any kids?"

Running his left hand down the side of his face he fought the urge to tell her to change the subject. His quick glance at her had their eyes locking briefly before he turned back to the road. "One. My son, Adam."

She nodded and turned to look out the windshield. Her voice grew softer, "How old is he?"

Now he had to swallow his own lump. "He's forever four."

She twisted in the seat and looked at him. His eyes darted to her then back to the road and he felt his nose begin to tingle as if the tears might come. Sniffing once he stared at the road. "Car accident. His mother was drunk and driving with him in the backseat. She hit a ditch and flipped the car. Bitch survived, Adam didn't."

Her words came out as whispers. "I'm sorry." Silence followed for a long while before she turned to him again. "So when you and Ford said, "For Adam", you're working to make him proud?"

All he could do was nod. Proud, make up for him getting killed, helping his grandparents out who loved him so much, all of it.

22

THEIR FIRST REAL TEST

Wow. If she were Dodge she'd have killed the bitch who killed his son. She was going to kill the bastard who killed her brother. Then she wondered how it all ended with his ex but wasn't sure it was something she should ask. Before she could screw up the courage, the Beast slowed before them and she looked out her window to the right.

Mags's house looked just like it did in the pictures Gaige had shown them. Perched high up on a hill, about three to four hundred yards from the road sat her palatial home. The flowers looked as they had in the pictures which meant they were fairly recent and likely from a drone nearby. GHOST worked with local law enforcement when they could. Pulling up her phone she tapped the icon for Wyatt, then the speaker icon and waited for his answer.

"Yeah."

"Gaige's pictures looked recent based on what I'm seeing now. Did he get drone footage from our friendly?"

"Not sure. Why does it matter?"

"Because, I'm guessing that Mags isn't the one taking care of that lush landscaping around her home. Everything looks perfect. So in some of that footage, I wonder if there was a lawn crew working here. Maybe a couple of us can go in as landscapers and check things out around the grounds."

"That's fabulous, Jax. Let me find out what I can from Gaige. Out."

She tapped the camera icon on her phone and readied it to snap pictures. At the same time, she pulled her lip gloss microphone from her bag and twisted the cap to turn it on. Rolling her window down she put her lip gloss in her mouth to hold it and aimed her camera at the fence and posts along the perimeter of the property as they drove slowly past. After Mags's property was out of sight, she tapped her phone again and uploaded the recording from her microphone. Once she finished she explained to Dodge.

"This microphone can pick up the sounds from a security system. It emits vibrations as it works. We'll know if Mags has one in a few minutes."

Dodge chuckled again. "I can't wait to get my hands on some of these gadgets."

"Usually you wouldn't be on missions with us until you saw all the goodies, but this whole thing happened fast because of circumstance. Once we finish this mission, you'll all get your own goodies. Our designer is good and will fit something that will work for you. Smokers get little lighters - though we don't have any now. My dad was a smoker and I still have his lighter, but I don't use it. He'll interview you and figure it all out. I have a compact in my duffle that's a camera. Josh and Wyatt have buttons on their shirts for a reason." She smiled at the look on his face. "I even have a pair of earrings that are cameras."

"That's so fucking amazing." They wove through the Ozark mountains a few miles before her phone rang.

She answered it with the speaker on. "Hi Gaige, what'cha got?"

"I hope answers to your questions. Yes, Mags uses a landscaping company and they're scheduled to come out every day to water, prune, and deadhead the flowers and perennials. Twice a week they mow and luckily for us that's today around noon. So, they'll come in three man crews. Josh and Ford are going in with them today to look around. I've got it worked out with the landscaping company and they're eager to cash the big bonus they'll be receiving. Josh and Ford will be on the mowers so they can travel the entire property, or at least the parts that are mowed. You, Dodge, and Wyatt will be on the perimeter hiding and they'll swing by with intel as they have it so you can report back to me. There's a barn on the grounds, hidden from the road that I want you three to get inside if you can and see what's in there. The guys will help you get on the grounds unseen. Take pictures and audio. Go in armed just in case."

Dodge nodded his head as Gaige spoke, which made her smile. He was ready and so was she. Dodge then asked, "Any signs of Mangus in these parts?"

"Not yet. But Lincoln and Hawk just saw his deep red Buick leaving town. We've got a drone following him for as far as we can, which will only be about fifty miles, but we suspect he's on his way down to the Ozarks. I'll let you know when we get confirmation of that. We've managed to secure three informants in the area. Farmers who are sick of the extortion. We're hoping to get a few more."

"That's perfect." She smiled as it seemed that things were coming together for them.

Gaige finished, "Great intel this morning you two. I've managed to clean the audio file you got. Mags has that diamond and they are planning to cut it up and sell it off in pieces. Keep your eyes peeled for signs of a cutting operation. That could be anything from a small living quarters where they'd keep the jeweler, trucks coming and going, crates and packages shuffling from location to location or anything similar."

"What about ordering a hit, did she do that, too?" She had to ask.

"Yes. Someone named Stan. He's not complying she said."

"Stan!" She swallowed and looked at Dodge. "The old man we met in the square?"

He cleared his throat. "Any description or details about who Stan is? We met a Stan this morning. He looked to be well into his eighties and he didn't speak to highly of Mags. Seems he owns a small country store in the square in Kingsdale, just across from Mags's restaurant."

"No description. Just that she needed the area secured and Stan wasn't complying."

Her heart dropped. He seemed nice enough and in some weird way she wondered if he'd approached them as a way to reach out to someone. Anyone.

Her voice softened. "Dodge, we need to go back and see if we can talk to him. He might have information for us if he's the Stan she's targeting and we might be able to save him."

He looked away from the road long enough to lock

eyes with her. She saw him swallow then look to the road again. It was a brief moment before he said, "Okay."

"You two stay safe and check in. By just after noon, you need to be in the back of Mags's property to get intel from Josh and Ford."

"Okay." She ended the call and looked straight ahead. "We have two hours to get to Kingsdale and back."

She pulled up a map of Kingsdale on her phone and searched for an alternate way in. "Here, I've got a back way and it looks like it comes in alongside Stan's store. So, maybe there's parking in the back."

"That's great, Jax." He turned down the first road that took them back to Kingsdale and her heart began to race. This could be their first real test as a team, though they'd managed so far. And this could bring them one step closer to Mangus.

23

WYATT CHUCKLED, THE FUCKER

"Okay, right here we're a bit hidden and still have easy access to get out." Dodge pulled into a spot behind Stan's store and off to the right. The area was unmoved and tall weeds stood all around. They didn't quite cover the car, but they camouflaged it well enough. Clearly there wasn't any traffic to speak of in this town, so they should be good parking here.

"Perfect." Jax twisted in her seat and looked the area over. When she turned back to him, her eyes sparkled and her smile was brilliant. "Let's do this."

He chuckled at her excitement. It was invigorating and a bit daunting. They needed to ensure they didn't screw this up. He took in a deep breath as he checked his ankles for his guns. One Springfield 9mm and one Ruger 380. Quietly getting out of the car and gently pushing the door closed, he opened the trunk and pulled his third pistol, a Ruger 9mm, from his bag and tucked it into the hidden holster in the front pocket of his jeans.

Jax followed much the same routine, she had two ankle holsters, hidden by her sexy ass-hugging jeans, and a holster in her bra. He'd be lying if he said he didn't want to see that one. Pulling the lid of the trunk down and pushing it closed, they inched along the back of the building.

An unfamiliar voice could be heard from the door. "Mags is a bit disappointed in you, Stan. You said you'd do your part and yet you turned away a shipment yesterday. So now she's of a mind that she doesn't need you anymore. You know what that means?"

He looked back at Jax and her lips were pinched together. She pointed to the backdoor and swirled her finger signaling he should go around to the front. He couldn't let her go in there alone. He shook his head and she vigorously nodded, then reached for the handle of the door.

"It means fuck Mags is what it means." Stan responded to his visitor.

An eerie laugh echoed out.

"Fuck." She muttered before she opened the door and stepped inside.

Indecision flooded his brain - follow her in or go around. Deciding to run around to the front of the store as she asked, he high stepped it around the store, hearing a gunshot just as he got to the door. Bursting through the front door, he quickly ducked behind shelving off to his right and out of range of the backdoor.

Another shot rang out and then a third one, the bullet whizzing past his head and hitting some old dusty bottles on the shelf behind him and then a fourth shot. Pulling his gun from his pocket he slowly squat-walked down the aisle, listening for more sounds.

A scuffle could be heard followed by a grunt and then a body hitting the floor. Something that sounded like a punch or a kick and then another grunt. Quickly making his way to the back, his breathing shallowed and his heart pounded, he found Jax, sitting on the chest of a younger man, at least younger than Mags and there was blood on his shirt near his stomach, just below Jax's ass. Stan leaned against a stack of boxes, holding his side, blood seeping between his fingers.

"I've got this piece of shit." Jax spat out and he chuckled a little - he'd been in that position and knew how strong she was. Relief sweeping through him, he holstered his gun then went to Stan, eased his hand away to see a bullet hole in the bib of his overalls. Pulling the denim away from his frail frame, the flannel shirt he wore had a matching hole. "I gotta look at this Stan, okay?"

"Yeah, go ahead. It didn't hit anything vital, your girl-friend got here in time to distract him." His old faded blue eyes flicked to Jax and his lips hitched up at the corners.

"Yeah, she's quick." And she was, and brave as fuck. She didn't hesitate to run into what could have been a deadly situation to save an old man she only just met.

Lifting Stan's shirt he saw the bullet had entered the flesh of his left side, just below his ribs. Feeling around his back, there was an exit wound which Dodge expected, since there wasn't much bulk to Stan to stop a bullet. "Let's get you sitting down, Stan."

Seeing an old wooden chair in the corner, he leaned Stan on the wall, nodded and grinned when he got a wink in return. He pulled the chair over to Stan and helped the old man sit down. Pulling his phone out he called Wyatt, "We've got Stan, need an ambulance and a cop. Two men hit with bullets, Stan and one of Mags's boys."

"Fuck." The man Jax sat on wheezed out. "She thought you two were suspicious."

Not words he wanted to hear. His eyes landed on Jax and her little nose wrinkled. She added a bit of pressure to the man's throat though he wasn't sure if it was to shut him up or make him pass out. Leaning back a bit she must have hit a tender spot from the gunshot wound and he groaned.

"Yeah, if he can be found, send him." He didn't want to give up their friendly's name in case this asshole got back to Mags before they finished their mission. One was certain, Mags was on to them, or at least suspicious of them now, and this wasn't going to help.

Mags's boy heaved up, trying to roll Jax off. She tightened her hold on his neck and reared back with her fine ass and put pressure on his stomach again. He groaned again and struggled to breathe.

"May as well kill him. We're all dead if he tells Mags what happened in here." Stan said.

Tucking his phone into his pocket, Dodge heaved out a breath, "Yeah, maybe we should but we'd rather take him in for questioning and see what he'll tell us."

Mags's boy finally passed out or so it seemed. Jax said over her shoulder, "I need something to tie him up with, I'm not getting off until he's secured."

Dodge ran through the store and rummaged for some rope. He found a bundle and went to the back of the store, tying the assailant's feet, and then motioning for Jax to get off him. Dodge rolled the man over and tied his hands behind his back. For good measure, he ran a length of rope between the man's hands and down through his ankles and around the rope at his feet, tying it off tightly.

"Wow, nice." Jax smiled.

"Hate to take chances."

He wanted to get what information he could from Stan. "Does Mags own the ambulance crew or anyone at the hospital?"

"Nah, the hospital is more than thirty miles away and she doesn't reach that far. She stays fairly close to this area and a little bit in Jasperville."

"How far is she into Jasperville?"

"Just a couple of places, the hotel and one little bar called Charlie's."

Stan coughed then winced and Dodge hated to ask him anymore.

Jax pulled her phone from her back pocket and walked to the backdoor. Tapping an icon, she listened until her brother answered.

"We broke up a potential murder. Trouble is I shot and wounded the asshole. And I'm afraid if he goes to the hospital they'll let him go or Mags will have people to get to him and find out what happened here. Think we can take him and question him somewhere to see what we can get out of him?"

Dodge looked around and decided to lock the front door so no one came in. No doubt someone heard the shots. Mags will think it was her boy shooting Stan for a while, but when he didn't go back, Dodge sure didn't want another of her errand boys coming in and causing trouble.

Walking through the front of the store he mused at the condition. It looked just like an old country general store, including the dust. Old Stan didn't do much around here including cleaning. The store looked more like a collection in someone's basement or attic.

Another shot rang out, and Dodge's heart hammered.

"Jax!" he shouted as he ran to the back of the store, his gun pulled and at the ready.

There he saw Stan standing over Mags's boy, with his gun dangling from his hand.

"I told you, you couldn't let him live."

Jax stood silent immediately inside the backdoor, her eyes locked on his her phone dangling from her fingers. He saw her swallow, then jerk her head as if to shake herself awake. Slowly she walked to Stan and put her hand over his gun hand.

"I need the gun, Stan.

The old man gave it up without a fuss. She took it and stepped away from him, laying the gun on the top of some crates. She looked at Dodge again and slightly nodded. He'd stood frozen at the thought she'd been shot and then trying to get his brain to catch up with the events of what had just happened.

Stan wheezed and he quickly walked to the old man. "Stan, sit down."

"It doesn't matter about me now, I'm a dead man anyway." He wheezed as he sat.

Jax knelt on one knee in front of Stan, "Don't say that. We'll get you out of here, Stan."

The old man's faded blue eyes locked on Jax's eyes and she softly smiled at him. "I have cancer sweetheart, I don't have long for this world anyway. It's the only reason I had the courage to stand-up to the old bitch. I was sick of her telling me what to do and when to do it."

She frowned at Stan's health news and several thoughts came to his mind at once. Even frowning she was beautiful, her clear olive skin radiant. Her dark brown eyes sparkled with the threat of tears and that's when it hit him. She tries being a hard ass, but she's just a softy inside. Sad for an old man she just met and his situation.

Jax took Stan's hands in hers and looked into his eyes. "Do you know anything about a large pink diamond or a jeweler somewhere in the area to cut it?"

Stan took a breath and nodded his head. "Yeah. She's got her at the hotel in Jasperville. I'm sure she'll be moving her today though. She wanted me to hide her at my house this week and that's the shipment I refused. So, she'll install her at one of her minion's house."

Dodge stepped forward, "Do you know which one? Does she look for anything in particular when stashing someone like the jeweler away?"

The elder man shrugged. "My house is only a mile from here and yet private. I live in the woods, just south of here."

Jax looked at him then and he suspected they were thinking the same thing, they'd likely passed his house on their way to Jasperville.

"Stan, do you live alone?" She squeezed his hands in hers.

"I've been all alone for the past many years. Martha, my wife, and I only had one son and they were both killed in a car accident years ago."

Jax turned to him. "So he's alone and close-by. That would mean no one else to worry about saying anything and close if she needs to get to him for any reason."

A truck could be heard outside and Dodge skirted past Jax and Stan and peeked out the backdoor. "Wyatt."

He opened the backdoor and nodded at Wyatt. The big man stepped into the store, looked around at the body on the floor and the old wheezing man sitting in a chair with blood all over his bibs and let out a whistle.

Moving to stand behind Jax he lowered his voice. "Stan, is the store next to you empty as it looks?"

Jax looked back at him, her brows furrowed.

"Yep. Alex Branson inherited it from his parents when they died. He tried opening some exercise place, but..." He laughed, then coughed. "Well, you know. There's no one to come and use it. He thought it would be his field of dreams."

Looking at Wyatt he said, "Let's move this body into that empty store until the cops come and go. We take Stan out of town with us and get him to the hospital in Jasperville, then we sit and wait. We can call cops about the body tomorrow or something. We just need Mags to think her plan to kill Stan worked."

Jax stood, her forehead wrinkled briefly. "You think she'll take the jeweler to Stan's now that she thinks he's dead?"

He nodded and smiled at her as her smile grew.

"Rather than taking Stan away..." She glanced at Stan and nodded. "What if our friendly pronounces him dead and word gets out? She'll certainly feel bold enough to use his house then."

She was smart this one.

She knelt in front of Stan again, "That is if you don't mind pretending to be dead as the ambulance carries you out Stan. Once you get to the hospital we'll have someone we trust sneak you out of the hospital in Jasperville and to another one where Mags won't know where you are."

Stan's wrinkled face beamed as he looked into Jax's eyes. "You folks are smart." He tapped her nose with his forefinger. "Especially you."

He looked at Dodge then. "You keep this one, she's priceless."

Wyatt chuckled, the fucker.

24

WATCHING THE BOYS MOW

She was going to chew him out for questioning her decision to go in the backdoor alone earlier, but then he came up with the brilliant idea to move the body. He looked fabulous doing it and when he smiled at her, she melted - just a little bit. The split second she was pissed at him, Stan needed her and she didn't have the time to stew on it like she normally would have. Maybe there was a lesson there, but she wasn't looking for self-help right now, she just wanted to complete their mission especially killing Mangus, make some big cash, and set herself up for a pleasant future, whatever that looked like.

So, Dodge and Wyatt moved Mags's boy's body through the door that connected Stan's store to the empty store. That was a handy little tidbit Stan shared with them. He had it hidden behind some tall shelves, which luckily the two strong men easily moved aside wide enough to carry the body through. She sat with Stan who was looking tired and she wondered for about the third or fourth time where the hell the ambulance was.

Dodge and Wyatt came through the connecting door, slid the shelves in place, and stacked some crates over the scuff marks on the floor where the shelving unit slid away from the wall.

Dodge's eyes met with hers and he nodded. She once again admired the green of his eyes. The brightness of them against the tanned skin of his face and the sandy blond of his hair was fabulously stunning. Even more stunning was the way his shirt stretched across the expanse of his chest and the outline of his abs showed against the soft t-shirt material, then tucked into the waistband of his jeans and looked oh-so-yummy. She'd always admired a firm muscled body.

Sirens sounded in the distance and she blinked quickly as the realization of what that meant dawned on her. Looking at Stan she knelt in front of him again. "Stan, the ambulance is coming. We have an officer coming, too, but he's not on Mags's payroll, he's a friendly. So, he'll make it look like he's investigating a murder scene, which he is, but he doesn't exactly know that. We hate to put him in too much trouble. But, you'll need to lay perfectly still when the ambulance takes you out. Can you do that?"

His wrinkled face stretched into a smile again. "Sure I can."

"Okay, but then after the hospital staff has stitched you up, we'll have a different ambulance come and take you to another hospital. We've got this, okay?"

His old voice was soft when he responded. "Honey, you don't need to worry about me. I'm at peace with all that has happened. I'm happy I stood up to her and I'm happy I killed her asshole lackey."

She smiled at the old man's pluck. "Good to hear." She

stood then asked one more question of Stan. "Where will you go when you get out of the hospital?"

He shrugged, "I don't have long. My sister lives about forty miles from here, I'll go there."

The sirens grew louder and finally stopped out front of the store. Wyatt walked to the front door to let them in and ushered them to the back.

She stood next to Stan as the ambulance crew came in with their gurney. Within a minute their friendly walked into the store and to the back with the rest of them.

"Folks, I'm looking for Jax and Dodge."

"That's us." She nodded to Dodge.

"I'm Officer Gerzek. I understand we have a sensitive situation here. Gaige Vickers spoke to me earlier and filled me in. These are friendlies also." He pointed at the EMTs. " Kevin and Jamie." Both men nodded as they got to work on Stan. Laying him on the gurney, they checked vitals and the bullet wound. Jamie looked up and said, "We need to administer antibiotics and an IV."

Dodge spoke quietly. "We need to make it appear as though he's dead for on-lookers. So, you'll need to wait on the antibiotics and IV until you get him into the ambulance."

Officer Gerzek nodded. "I'll fill you guys in at the hospital. Okay, let's go." He looked at Dodge then, "How are things playing out with you two? They're going to want to know who called the cops and ambulance."

Wyatt spoke up, "Me. Mags hasn't seen my face yet and I can claim to be a customer who wandered into town. My SUV is out back."

Wyatt looked at her then Dodge, "You two need to get lost before I show my face."

She looked at Stan and took his frail hand in hers. "I'll be checking in on you, Stan."

He nodded, then pulled his wallet out of the front pocket on his uninjured side. Flipping it open he said, "Here's my address, you go look there later and see if that bitch has your jeweler in my house." He leaned back and caught his breath. "I have a key in the top drawer of the til. Just press the "esc" button and it'll open."

Jax pulled her phone from her back pocket and snapped a picture of Stan's driver's license. Then she asked, "Where's your car, Stan?"

He smiled. "I parked it across the square behind the yoga place. That's where I was walking from this morning when I saw you two kissing in the square."

Wyatt snorted then chuckled. Dodge glanced at her before she looked back to Stan. She'd deal with Wyatt later. "Why do you park over there?"

"I park at all different places every day. I never want Mags knowing exactly where to look for me."

She giggled then. The old man had spunk. "You take care, Stan and we'll watch out for your house and you."

"Just get that bitch." He wheezed.

Kevin started moving the gurney. "We've got to get going folks."

Dodge opened the backdoor and waited for her to exit the store. Wyatt chuckled again and she punched him in the stomach on her way out. Not hard enough to hurt him, just enough to shut him up. She passed Dodge and made her way to the car, her eyes looking over the back of the store and the area to see if she could see anyone.

Climbing into the passenger side of the car, she pulled her door closed quietly. Dodge wasn't far behind her and quickly started the car up and backed away from the building. Turning down the side road he exited town the back way they had come in.

He glanced at her briefly, "What's Stan's address? We'll go past it and see if there's any activity before we go and watch Ford and Josh mow Mags's lawn."

She looked at him and the smile on his face was swoon worthy. His eyes met hers and they both busted up laughing. That was kind of funny.

She read the address to him and then put it into the map app on her phone. "There it is."

The dirt driveway led to a little white house, neatly mowed. No cars showed in the drive but of course they couldn't see into the garage and they weren't going to stop during the day.

She sat back in the seat, "Wanna bet she's bringing the jeweler here?"

"Yep, I think that's exactly what she's going to do. Stan's out of the way, she'll wonder about her boy, but Wyatt'll take care of that. She doesn't stop business for any lackey going missing, that's my guess."

Okay, she'd give Dodge the jeweler and the pink diamond 'cause that looked like it was going to happen and soon. Then, tomorrow she'd get Mangus. Things were looking up for her.

Her phone rang, she looked at the screen then announced. "Gaige." She tapped the answer icon then the speaker icon.

"Hi Gaige, Dodge and I are here."

"Great job on Stan. Wyatt filled me in. He saw Mags waddling across the square to see if she could get a look at Stan, but our guys quickly got him inside and took off. She asked Wyatt what happened and he said he came in to buy some antiques for his mom and just as he walked in some guy shot and killed Stan then ran out the backdoor."

"Did she believe him?"

"He said she was hard to read, but she has nothing to go on just yet. No doubt she went back to the cafe and tried calling her minion, but Dodge disassembled his phone when they took him next door. So, she'll only get voicemail."

She looked over at Dodge but he just looked straight ahead. Damn man was good.

She responded to Gaige. "Okay, we're on our way out to Mags's now to watch the boys mow." She laughed and Dodge and Gaige both chuckled.

25

CLEAR

.

Dodge hunkered down behind a triple-wide fence post at the farthest point from Mags's house. The temperature had certainly risen ten degrees or more and he'd begun sweating. Tapping the ear piece, he called out to his team. "I'm in place."

His earpiece cracked once and Jax's voice sounded. "I'm in place, too."

The mower Josh was on came close to his location, but Josh turned and headed back toward the house, keeping his mow lines straight. Dodge could see him and watched as he acted as if he was scratching his head. "There was activity in the barn about an hour ago, but that has since died off. A blue pickup pulled away from there but I couldn't see inside."

Tapping his earpiece, he replied. "Roger. I'll check it out."

Another crack before Ford added, "I could see them loading a couple of crates and strangely a suitcase into the back of the truck."

"Roger." He replied. Easing his way back down the

path he'd come up, he turned east and toward the barn. The weeds outside the fence were tall enough that he had coverage as he crawled along the ground. The dust he managed to disturb and the bugs whose resting spots he interrupted flurried around his face and ears. Damn it, he hated that the most.

The fragrance of the fresh-mowed grass wafted over to him and he inhaled deeply. That was an amazing smell. It reminded him of being a boy, playing in the yard with his friends on a hot summer day back home. He was a southern boy, born and raised. Then he joined the Army and lived everywhere in a short amount of time. Deployed to Bosnia and Indonesia. He'd lost his accent. Mostly because he hated being teased about it, so he consciously learned to speak without one. Then he'd gone back, close to home in Alabama and dove into the police work. But, he vowed to keep his accent at bay.

Stopping every few feet to listen for anything unusual and certainly for snakes. He hated snakes. With a passion. He continued on his crawl til he was directly across from the barn. The fence could certainly be breached, it was mostly there to give the impression of being impenetrable, the issue was that there was more than forty yards from the fence to the barn and it was all mowed and cleared.

Tapping his earpiece he asked to anyone listening. "Any ideas how to get into the barn from the field undetected?"

Josh responded. "Go to the far east side of the barn and wait. I have a full bag of grass to dump on that side and to do that, we have to open the gate, drive the mowers out, dump the clippings on the trailer and then drive back in. Don't ask why, it's a stupid rule of hers. But, in the meantime, the trailer will block your path and the mower will hide your entry into the barn. There are two guards walking the wrap-around porch watching us all the time, so I won't be able to dally."

"Roger."

Continuing around to the far east of the barn he spied the work truck that read, Delgado Lawn Service with the trailer attached to it parked just outside of the gate. He couldn't see the house from here, with the barn in the way. Looking up and around he spotted electronics hanging from the soffit of the barn at each corner.

Asking into his wire, "I thought there wasn't a security system in place? I see cameras or electronics hanging from the barn."

Ford responded. "They're fake. The lawn manager shared that with us on the sly."

Dodge inched as close as he dared to the edge of the field and Josh added, "But, those guards on the porch have a vantage point and can see easily down the hill so keep your head low. They are most interested in the barn."

Faint rustling caught his attention from behind and he swung his head around to see Jax, crawling toward him. What actually caught his attention was Jax's cleavage, which showed beautifully as she crawled toward him, her white tank top hanging low. Her side to side movements made her breasts sway and he swallowed the lump in his throat. He needed to go bang some piece of ass in town and soon, his carnal thoughts continued in Jax's direction and that couldn't happen.

"Eyes up here, buddy." She said when she looked up at him.

He turned toward the barn and she inched up along-side him. In the heat her scent magnified and dammit she smelled good. Almost musk and cinnamon mixed. Fuck.

"Don't wear low cut tanks if you don't want men looking."

She clucked her tongue but said nothing in response. "You men are so fucking easy. It's a wonder any of you ever get out of a situation alive. All it takes is a tit or an ass and you're all mesmerized."

His earpiece cracked. "On my way to the truck now, get in position." Josh called out.

Raising himself up on his haunches, he readied himself to run and Jax did the same. "What do you think you're doing?"

Her voice lowered, "Going in to investigate the barn. It's a big building and we don't have a lot of time. Seems all activity out here is centered on this place."

He heaved out a breath, "Jax..."

"Nope - stop second-guessing me. Stop trying to argue. Just stop."

He muttered, "Jesus."

Jax sighed and it irritated him this time.

The sound of the mower grew louder. Josh appeared at the gate, opened it up, and slowly drove the mower to the trailer just outside of the gate. Entering through the gate he jumped on the mower and drove it to the trailer. He quickly tapped his comm and said, "As soon as I finish dumping the clippings, I'll drive back into the gate and that would be the time to hunker down alongside and run into the barn."

Josh dumped his clippings into a neat pile on the trailer, which was an impressive rig. Large to minimize the time it took to mow her five acres, the large bagging attachment on the back of the mower would indeed hide them as they ran to the barn. Getting into place along the mower as Josh finished with the clippings he locked eyes with Josh. A slight nod from his teammate was the only acknowledgement he got. It was all he needed.

Josh hopped back on the mower and Dodge ran alongside until the point he and Jax could slip in behind the barn. Edging their way along the backside he found a door and pulled it open just enough to slip inside. Jax pulled the door closed behind her and he stood still until his eyes adjusted to the lack of light.

The smell of hay filled his nostrils and soft shuffling could be heard on the far side. Listening further the sounds of hooves tapping the ground eased his tension and he let out a long-held breath. Inching along the wall he neared the center of the barn where he could see support beams holding up the mow floor every few yards or so. Easing to one, he pushed his back to it and peered around. Jax lay her hand on his shoulder and squeezed once before inching past him and to the next post. With hand signals he motioned to the far side of the barn and pointed to himself. She nodded and disappeared into the darkness on the other side. Taking in another deep breath he wrestled with letting her go alone. It was against everything he was trained to do as a child. "Men are on earth to help protect women, son." He could still hear his father's voice telling him that.

Giving his head a slight shake he entered the darkness on his side of the barn, thankful for the light that seeped in between the boards on the barn every few feet. A door opened a few feet from him and he could see a well-lit area behind it with what looked like horse stalls. Two men could be heard talking and shovels scraping the floor drown them out. Pressing his back against the nearest beam he waited until one man grabbed a bale of straw, and went back into the lit area.

As soon as the door closed he made progress toward that doorway to hopefully slip inside.

His earpiece cracked once and Wyatt said, "I'm in place at the far west of the property."

Ford responded to him, "Dodge and Jax are inside the barn investigating now, edge closer to the barn in case they need help."

"Roger." Wyatt responded and he hoped like hell that sound didn't leech out of his earpiece so anyone in the barn could hear.

The door opened again and Dodge pressed his back against a beam. This time he could see the same man exit the room, he wore a blue denim long sleeved shirt, cowboy boots that tapped along the concrete floor, and jeans. He had a brown cowboy hat perched on his head which almost made Dodge chuckle. The man wasn't more than five foot four inches tall or so. He looked like a tiny cowboy. The cowboy grabbed another bale of straw and twisted to go back to the room. His eyes landed on Dodge and he held his breath. Slowly the man set his straw on the ground and inched his way toward Dodge. Two steps toward Dodge the man yelled and reached around his back and quickly pulled a gun. Dodge pulled his gun from his pocket and shot. The man fell back into the straw, but the noise raised a ruckus in the stable area and the door burst open. Three men poured out of the stable door, yelling in Spanish. Dodge turned to the door and leveled his gun on the first man of the three out. Heart hammering, sweat running down his back, he hated having to shoot people. But, it was fight or die and that man pulled on him. Now he stood eye to eye with three men. One in the back, slowly reached behind him and he knew what that meant. The glint of metal as it lifted through the light shaft between the barn boards caught his attention and he yelled, "Freeze."

Luckily the man did as he was told, but the first man out said something to the other two and the second man's lips turned into a sickening smile. The first man yelled, "Disparar." His Spanish was limited but he knew that one and it meant shoot.

Gun fire rang out and a burning sensation ripped through his left shoulder but he continued to shoot and duck behind the support beam he was so very grateful for. The three men lay on the ground a few feet away from the short man, but he only remembered shooting that one.

Jax came running to his side, "We've got to get out of here, the guards will be coming." He stood to move and the room spun around. Grabbing Jax for support she swung her head to look at him then spit out, "Fuck."

Tucking herself under his right arm she helped him from the middle of the barn to the backdoor where they'd come in. Stopping for a split second she tapped her ear comm. "Wyatt, I need help, Dodge has been shot."

"I heard the gunshots. I'm at the backdoor."

Light shown into the barn as the backdoor opened and he struggled to keep up with Jax as she practically dragged him from the barn.

"Fuck buddy, what the hell?" Wyatt grabbed him by the front of the shirt and Jax quickly ducked under his arm as Wyatt took over from there. The fresh air helped him regain his equilibrium and he snapped out of his haze.

"Okay, I'm good. Needed air."

"Well, hang on, I'm not letting go." Running along the back of the barn their ear comms cracked and Ford yelled, "Get out now. Take the landscaping truck and go."

Wyatt practically threw him into the backseat and Jax climbed in behind him. Wyatt jumped into the driver's seat and took off. Bullets rained over the top of the truck, Jax lay across his chest and a bullet went through the back window, exiting the front passenger side of the windshield. Wyatt stepped on the gas and they flew down the driveway. Once he turned onto the road he yelled back to them, "Clear."

26

HE'S LOSING BLOOD

"Okay, lay still." She looked over the front seat. "Can you check the glove box and see if there's a first aid kit?"

"Hang on."

The truck lurched back and forth as Wyatt leaned over and opened the glove box. "Nothing."

Jax's head spun around, checking under the seat and behind it as much as she could.

"Fuck." She didn't yell, but they weren't prepared for an issue like this. If they had the Beast, they'd be prepared. As if Wyatt knew what she was thinking, he turned down a side road and pulled the truck into a cleared area in the woods. Slamming the shifter into Park, he opened the door and jumped out. Looking back at her he said, "The Beast is just up this road, not far." She followed the direction his arm pointed. "I'm going to get it. Get Dodge sitting up and ready to transfer as soon as I get back."

She nodded. When she turned to Dodge he had a slight grin on his face. "What are you smiling at?"

"You're worried about me."

"Of course I'm worried you idiot, you've been shot. Though it's not life threatening, you sure don't want it to get infected."

"I think you care a little bit, Jax."

She wasn't going to answer him. Did she care. Sure. Of course. Who wouldn't. Right? But, she didn't care, care. Not like that.

His right hand grasped her left arm and slightly squeezed. "Jax?"

"Stop it. What's wrong with you?"

"I've been shot."

"I know that you jerk. I mean, don't talk all that mushy bullshit."

He laughed then. His face transformed when he laughed. And, shit there was a dimple in his cheek. Crap, both of them. She'd not noticed that before. Double shit. His full lips, curved perfectly and his teeth which were flawless and white made him look like a prince. His green eyes sparkled and her traitor of a heart sped up when she remembered those fascinating lips touching hers.

"You care. You're just too stubborn to admit it."

"I'm not stubborn."

He laughed again, a full on belly laugh. He moved to sit up then and grabbed the back of the seat as he seemed to become dizzy from the effort.

"Tell me what's going on Dodge. Your shoulder is bleeding but not enough for you to be dizzy from loss of blood. Were you hit anywhere else?" She examined his shoulder for an exit wound and found one. That was good.

He let out a deep breath and ran his right hand along

his face. "No, it's just the adrenaline leaving my body. Kind of a rush."

The Beast came into view and Dodge opened the door and stepped from the truck, though not all that gracefully. He hung onto the door handle until he could get his bearings. Damned stubborn man wouldn't even wait for her to help him.

Quickly scooting across the seat and jumping from the truck behind Dodge, she once again draped his right arm over her shoulders, firmly grasped his hand in hers, and wrapped her arm around his back as she led him to the edge of the road where Wyatt would stop the Beast to let them in. He leaned heavily on her and staggered a bit as she led him. Her gut told her something wasn't right, but Wyatt and Gaige were the medics of the team.

Wyatt stopped the Beast and she yelled, "I need some help with him."

Jumping from the truck, he had all 6'7" of his body next to her in no time. "Something's not right, Wyatt, it's like he must be losing blood internally. I'll drive while you work on him. I think we need to get him to a hospital."

Wyatt took over carrying Dodge to the Beast, hustled him into the backseat while she quickly climbed into the driver's seat. Adjusted the seat for the major height difference and took off without any other thought. Tapping her ear comm she said, "Gaige, we need directions to the closest hospital sent to the Beast."

"Report to me." Came his worried voice.

"Dodge was shot in Mags's barn. In the shoulder but it seems as though he's losing blood. Wyatt's got him now."

"Shit." Came over the comm but she wasn't sure whose voice it was. She practiced some deep breathing exercises and focused on the curving mountain roads. Last thing they needed was to crash.

Their comms cracked and Josh quickly reported. "Cops are here. We acted like you stole our work truck and we're all upset. Gonna owe Mr. Delgado a repair job and some cash for his troubles. Our friendly from the County Sheriff's office is among them. He showed when he heard the call come in. We'll be here a while as they investigate and get our story about the dead guys, and Mr. Delgado can get someone to come out here and pick us up. You still have his truck?"

She responded. "Nope, we left it just around the back of the hills behind Mags's where Wyatt stashed it. We're in the Beast."

She navigated a sharp curve and glanced into the mirror. All she could see was Wyatt looking down at Dodge and digging through their impressive first aid kit.

The ear comms chirped again. "Wyatt, can you report?" Gaige asked.

She watched him in the mirror quickly tap his comm. "I think his Brachial artery is nicked. The blood that's present is light in color. There's a lot of internal bleeding in his shoulder. It's pooling up behind the skin and he's groggy."

She swallowed the lump in her throat and blinked furiously at the tears that threatened to spill over her eyelids. He had to be okay. She sent up a silent prayer, *"Lord, let him be okay and I promise I'll be nicer to him. I care about him, and I'm attracted to him, too, but that doesn't mean anything where you're concerned, I just want him to be okay. Please."*

The computer on the Beast chimed and the GPS lit up, directions to the hospital in Jasperville appeared on the screen and according to that, they were only fifteen minutes away.

She sat straighter in the seat and swallowed a few times to moisten her throat. Swiping at the tears in the corners of her eyes she focused on the winding roads ahead and getting Dodge to the hospital.

27

IT WAS A START

He opened his eyes, or tried too. It seemed as if a pile of sand had been poured on them. Lifting his hands to rub the dryness away pain shot through his left shoulder and he gasped.

"Hey, be careful there." The bed dipped and Jax's voice grew closer. "You're going to be alright, Tarzan."

She placed a wet cloth over his eyes and lightly dabbed at them, then removed the cloth. "Anesthesia makes your eyes and throat dry. I can give you some ice chips."

"Yeah." He croaked out, his parched throat unrecognizable to himself.

Blinking his eyes open he watched Jax as she dumped some ice chips from the yellow plastic pitcher on the bedside table into the glass. Then unwrapped a plastic spoon and tossed the cellophane wrapper into a nearby wastebasket. Lifting some ice chips from the glass with the spoon, she held it to his lips and watched him closely as his lips closed around the spoon and took the chips of frozen water into his mouth. He inwardly smiled. She cared.

He let the chips melt in his mouth which took only a few seconds then swallowed.

"More?"

"Yeah."

She mirrored her motions, lifting the chips to his mouth. He watched her eyes absorb him. Her eyes moved to his and held for a moment before she said, "You were shot in the shoulder and the bullet nicked your Brachial artery. It was a small nick but it created a pinhole which leaked blood into your shoulder. It made you dizzy and you lost a lot of blood, not enough to endanger your life, since you have great teammates. Wyatt helped you and we got you to the hospital right away."

Her lips curved up into a serene smile, the corners of her eyes crinkled and for the first time he thought she looked absolutely beautiful. Not just attractive or pretty, but gorgeous. Her olive skin was flawless and fresh, the whites of her eyes bright which made the brown of her irises look dark and mysterious. He remembered her lips and how they felt against his and it made him smile.

"Great teammates? Is that how this is going to go? I'm never going to hear the end of this again because you had to get me to safety?"

She snickered and it was the most pleasant sound. "There may come a day when you'll hear the end of it." She moved to set the cup on the table and that's when he noticed the front of her shirt had blood on it. "But not anytime soon."

She looked at her shirt when she saw the direction of his gaze. "It's your blood from when I lay over you in the back of the truck as we were driving away."

Slowly nodding his head he cleared his throat. "I remember."

"Okay. So, Gaige worked some magic and got you in a private room. But, we're planning on taking you back to the hotel tonight because we simply don't trust Mags and how far reaching she may be. We're in Jasperville now and it's not far enough away, so we're going back to Stangleville, where we stayed last night but to a different hotel. If we can get you released. You need to do your part. When the doctor comes in, he needs to see your vitals are good. Since Wyatt is a medic, he can take care of you and the doctor has already spoken to him. He knows the potential danger we're in, and frankly, they don't want us here any longer than we need to be because of it. Wyatt did a great job of patching you up and stifling the bleeding while we were in transit."

An ugly little jealousy gremlin jumped into his head. "You and Wyatt a thing?"

She raised one eyebrow and looked at him like he spoke in tongues.

"What?"

"You seem very fond of him and he you. I just wondered if you were a thing or if you had ever been a thing."

"Nope." She stood, hands on her hips and squared her shoulders. "And not that it's any of your business, but the only team member I've ever slept with is Hawk. One time and we both knew it was a mistake afterward and we've never slept together again. I'm not a pass-around girl, I don't sleep around, and mostly, I'm a professional. I didn't get my job by sleeping for it and I won't keep it that way, either."

"Easy, easy, easy." Wrestling with his tired body he sat

up in his bed, swung his legs over the side and looked at her. "I didn't mean that. I mean, I didn't mean to imply you were someone who slept around. Wyatt said something yesterday about what a spitfire you were and the way he said it I wondered if you and he had..." He shook his head then looked into her eyes. "Hawk?"

"Once."

"Right. None of my business. Except, I'm kind of making it my business."

He saw her swallow and fidget with her fingers. Her voice was soft when she replied, "Don't."

"Jax?" He slowly stood, holding onto the bedrail and afraid to move just yet. His knees felt a bit shaky and he didn't trust them. "Come here."

"Tarzan, don't hurt yourself."

"Come here."

She hesitantly stepped up to him and he placed his right hand on her shoulder.

"I think you care."

"Stop."

"I do, too, Little Mama. I care."

Her head tilted up to look him in the eye. She swallowed again then pulled her bottom lip between her teeth.

"I don't think this is a good..."

"What's going on in here?" Josh entered the room, Ford and Wyatt behind him. He didn't seem mad but the look he gave his sister meant there'd be a discussion later on.

"Dodge lost his balance and I was here to save him. Again." She giggled probably more to appease her brother than anything. "I think he's anxious to get out of here."

Swallowing again he took a breath. "If you can help me over to the chair, I'd like to put my pants and shoes on." It suddenly dawned on him that he was wearing a hospital gown and it seemed his underwear, thank God.

"Shouldn't you wait for the doctor to release you?" Ford walked up to him and wrapped one of his big arms around Dodge's waist to help him to the chair. Disappointment flooded through him that Jax wasn't tucked under his arm, but he had a feeling they'd have other opportunities in the future. That Little Mama cared. It was a start.

28

I'LL GO GET THE BEAST

"Okay, so I think we've got everything you need from the Beast." Dropping the last two duffle bags on the bed nearest the door, she glanced over at Dodge, who lay on the other queen sized bed in the hotel room and made it look small. She'd propped pillows behind his back as he lay on his side to take the pressure off his shoulder. The television was on but he was already nodding off.

Wyatt dug around in his duffle and nodded. "Okay. We'll be listening on the comm units here. I hope you find the jeweler, the diamond, and that fucker Mangus."

"That's the plan. I'll talk to you later." She glanced over to Dodge and he was fast asleep. That was good, it would help him heal, but if she were honest, she wanted him to tell her to be careful and good luck. Or maybe just a little kiss. Something.

She left their room and walked next door to Josh and Ford's room, knocked once and the door flew open. Josh stood in front of her with a scowl on his face.

"You and Dodge got something going?"

"It's none of your business."

"It is if it brings harm to the team."

"It won't bring harm to the team."

"These things have a way of spiraling out of control, Jax."

"Mind your own business, Josh."

She turned and stalked toward the elevator, she wasn't listening to his bullshit. Jabbing the down arrow on the wall she took in a deep breath as she heard Josh come to stand just behind her.

"I'm sorry." His voice was low.

Glancing over her shoulder she looked at her brother, her rock and her best friend. Ford had quietly joined them but stared straight ahead, not saying a word.

"It's okay. But, my love life, or lack of one, is no one else's business. I don't judge you or any of the guys for that matter, for who they are with or not. I'd appreciate the same courtesy."

She heard her brother's deep intake of breath. "I said I only worried because of the team."

Ford finally interjected. "Dodge would never do anything to hurt the team. And, for what it's worth, he's a good guy, he'd never get involved unless he had strong feelings."

Her eyes glanced at his. They were strangely dark, it was hard to tell where his pupil ended and the iris began, but she could see sincerity in them.

The elevator door opened and she stepped in and stood at the back of the elevator, time to get her head into their mission. She closed her eyes as they descended to the first floor and tried to get the images of Dodge out of her head. What was happening to her? She'd shut her brother down and in the same moment, allowed him to think there was something between her and Dodge. They'd shared a couple of kisses. Nothing more. And, she did care. Just a few days ago she hated him and was so damned mad at him, but that seemed like a distant memory now.

The doors slid open with a whoosh, and the threesome stepped out walking silently out to the Beast - time to rock.

She immediately climbed into the backseat while Josh and Ford jumped into the front. Reaching into the tool boxes in the back behind the seat she began pulling weapons and ammo. She'd reloaded her pistol from earlier today as soon as Dodge had been taken into surgery. Needing the distraction, she'd gone out to the Beast and reloaded, organized and kept herself busy for about a half hour. She'd also prayed he'd be alright. They'd not known each other long, but there was a pull between them. A thing. An indescribable something.

Checking that her pistols were all in place, she also tucked a small knife into her left ankle holster on the inside.

Ford opened the console between the driver and passenger seats and began pulling comm units out. Handing one back to her, she whispered, "Thanks." And tucked it behind her ear, draping the short wire behind her neck at her nape, and using a piece of tape Ford held for her, taped it in place. She took a deep breath and slowly let it out.

Josh called out, "Twenty-five minutes. Questions on the mission?"

"No." She replied, they'd gone over it before and doing it again would just make her nervous.

Ford replied in kind, then added. "Check, check."

Wyatt came over the comm first, "Copy."

Then Gaige. "Lincoln and I are here."

Her turn. "Check, check."

Both of their distance teams replied, "Copy."

She spent the next few minutes running their mission through her head and sending up a silent prayer or two that Dodge would get stronger soon. Tapping her cell phone to the "dark screen" mode, which wouldn't emit a bright light as she used their apps, she debated on sending Dodge a text, then told herself to play it cool.

Pulling onto a lane in the woods about a mile from Stan's house, Josh cut the lights and hooked up his comm unit. He went through the checks and opened his door.

She scooted out of the back, reaching in for the weapons she'd just readied and handed Ford his rifle; she walked around to the driver's side and handed Josh his. She slung hers over her shoulder with the strap.

Josh tapped her nose lightly, "Be careful, heads up, no superwoman moves, got it?"

"Same to you, brother. Ford."

She looked at each of them in turn and received nods in return. They entered the woods and split up, each of them going in a different direction to surround the house on three sides. She was a half-click out when her comm unit cracked. "Be careful, Little Mama. Comm units are all live now."

Her heart raced at the sound of Dodge's voice. She responded. "You got it, Tarzan."

She could feel the smile on her face and she allowed it to remain for a few moments. She wanted to bring that pink diamond back to him just as bad as she wanted Mangus. That was a thought that surprised the shit out of her. Shaking her head, she silently navigated the thick brush, listening for any sounds that told her she wasn't alone.

Nearing the edge of the woods, she knelt down and peered at Stan's house. Faint yellow light poured from the downstairs windows on this side of the house, the rest of the house was dark. She told her team, "Target in sight. Faint light from the lower east side windows. I can't see any cars from this vantage point. Over."

Ford replied first. "One female visible through the west windows, appears to be a living room. Only a small area visible. West side of upper is dark and there's one car, a white Ford Taurus in the drive, in front of the backdoor. Over."

Josh responded. "South side clear. I can see the Taurus, faint lights here, and using my looking glass one man visible downstairs, sitting at the table in the living room. Over."

Pulling her portable night vision goggles, which they called their "looking glasses", up she looked into the house through the lighted window. "I can see the one man sitting at a table, too. Man two walking the perimeter of the house - armed. Over."

Josh called out. "Proceed."

She eased herself from the woods and ran to the house, pushing her back against the closest wall. Listening for sounds that she'd been seen she waited and willed her heart to slow down. This was always the most exciting part. The hunt. The thrill of getting close to your prey undetected. The next best part was the look of surprise on their faces.

She pulled her cell phone from her back pocket and tapped the icon for detecting if they had a security system installed. Watching for any red glow showing her how strong a system they had, nothing came onto her screen. They wouldn't have had enough time to set one up, but you couldn't underestimate Mangus. She whispered, "No security."

"Proceed." Josh replied.

She eased along the side of the house, making her way to the front porch. Peeking around the corner, she waited to see if the armed man she'd seen walking the perimeter was patrolling this area and he wasn't. Easing herself up onto the porch, she again flattened her back to the wall and waited for Josh and Ford to signal that they were in place.

Seconds later, two signals happened in her headset, then two more. She tapped hers twice letting them know she was in place, turned, waited until she heard the back-door kicked open and the yelling. The guard watching the front turned and ran through the house to the commotion. She instantly entered the living room with her rifle raised in front of her.

Two shots rang out from the back while in the living room she saw a blond woman, sitting at a table, a large pink stone in front of her and cutting materials on the table. She wore headgear that looked to be lighted, magnifying goggles which she quickly raised with the back of her hand. Her eyes were large and round as she looked down the barrel of Jax's rifle and, if not for the seriousness of the situation, Jax would have chuckled. She just loved this part.

"Pack it all up. Quickly, but efficiently, and keep your hands where I can see them or I'll break them."

Her lips quivered slightly, but she began rolling the

soft cloth with the pink stone and the smaller pieces that lay in front of her. Jax's eyes landed on a black box laying alongside the table and she pointed to it saying, "Slowly open the lid on that box with your foot."

The woman did as she was told and a quick look inside showed it to be empty. "Put it in there. Quickly."

Moving as fast as her shaking hands would allow, the woman did as she was told. "Set it on the table."

With one hand Jax reached back and pulled zip ties from her back pocket. Ford walked into the room from the back and said to her. "Josh has her guards."

"Roger. You got her?"

"Yep."

Resting her gun on its strap she stepped to the woman, grabbed her hands, and zip tied them behind her back. She picked up the box, then saw strapping tape on a nearby table, she quickly wrapped tape around the box to secure the diamonds inside. Turning to look at Ford she nodded and he ordered the woman, "Move."

Jax grabbed her upper arm and lead her to the door. Josh stepped from the kitchen, his gun aimed at the blond woman. He nodded at Ford then slung his gun over his shoulder as he began rummaging through the boxes and bags laying around the living room. Searching the next room, which seemed to be Stan's bedroom, he came out with a suitcase. The blond woman's eyes grew large as she saw it. He grinned. Ford's eyes grew big, too.

"That suitcase was at the barn earlier today."

"Where's the guards?" Jax asked him.

"Dead." Josh said. "I'll go get the Beast and call Gaige."

29

WE'RE GOING BACK TO STAN'S

"We got the diamond and the jeweler." Her smile was large in her face; she could feel how her cheeks stretched when she relayed that message.

"Fucking A. Great job." Dodge called back. He sounded stronger and her heart fluttered in her chest. Ford and Josh chuckled in the front seat but kept talking to a minimum.

"Thanks." She replied. "We'll be back soon." Ford tapped the button to end the call on the dash.

They still had the jeweler, sitting next to her in the Beast, her hands still secured behind her back, to deal with. Turning to her, Jax tried striking up a conversation.

"My name's Jax what's yours?"

Even in the dark the woman's light blue eyes could be seen clearly. They surveyed Jax and uncertainty was clear in them. Her continued silence irritated Jax.

"You're not going back to Mangus. If you're worried about his wrath, you shouldn't, we've already got him in custody, now we're just wrapping things up. How do you think we knew you'd be at Stan's house?"

Those blue eyes turned to Ford, who stared straight ahead, then rested on Josh in the rearview mirror. His eyes caught hers, then shifted quickly to the road. Turning back to her, she whispered, "Georgia."

"Georgia. What's your last name Georgia?"

"Parks."

"Well, it's nice to meet you Georgia Parks." She twisted in her seat to look at Georgia directly. "That's Ford." She pointed to the front passenger seat. "And that's Josh." She pointed. Both men only nodded.

"You seem to have a bit of an accent but not from here, so let's start with that."

Georgia bit her bottom lip but never looked away. Jax kept eye contact but focused on keeping her expression friendly.

"I'm from South Africa."

"What on earth is a South African jeweler doing in Arkansas in someone else's house cutting up stolen diamonds?"

"My family needs the money. Mr. Santarino say he will pay me good."

"Okay. And is this the first time you've worked for Mr. Santarino?" It grated on her nerves to call him Mr. Santarino. That son of a bitch didn't deserve that amount of respect."

"No. I work for him sometimes. When he have something big. I'm the best cutter." She took a deep breath. "We need the money. My mother is sick and needs treatment. I do nothing wrong."

"Well actually you are doing something wrong. Mr.

Santarino does not own that pink diamond you were cutting up. It isn't his to cut up."

"No he told me all is good."

"He lied to you."

Ford tapped his comm and Gaige responded. "Gaige here."

"Our asset is in the dark. We need a place to stash her until we get our man."

"Hawk and Axel are on the way down. They left a couple hours ago. In the meantime, you can't very well take her to the hotel, so you'll need to sit with her in the Beast until they get there. They'll bring her back here."

Ford looked to Josh who swore under his breath. Ford tapped his comm. "How about we drop her at the jail in Stangleville?"

"No, I no go to jail. I no do wrong." Georgia pleaded.

Touching Georgia's shoulder she waited until Georgia looked at her. "You're not going to jail because you did something wrong. We just need to keep you safe until we're finished with our investigation."

"Let me go home please."

"We can't do that Georgia. Mr. Santarino knows where to find you and you won't be safe."

"You said you had him. That I am safe."

Squeezing Georgia's shoulder a bit, she replied. "We don't quite have him. But we will and soon. If you help us we can keep you safe."

"You lie to me."

"So did Mr. Santarino. He lied to you. You were cutting up stolen goods for him. Now you can work with us to keep you safe or we'll get word to him that you've told us enough information to prosecute him. Then, you'll be in danger and so will your family."

Tears sprang to her eyes and traveled down her cheeks. Jax turned in her seat to face forward. She'd not say anything to Georgia now until she started helping them with some information.

Their comms chirped and Lincoln said, "Stangleville jail is ready to receive our asset. Have Hawk and Axel ask for Sergeant Maxwell when they get there, he's been informed of the situation."

Ford responded. "Thanks, Linc. We're on our way there now and about twenty minutes out."

He then turned to Georgia and said, "We're taking you to jail."

Georgia sniffed loudly. "I'll help you."

Jax turned to her again. "Where is Mr. Santarino?"

"I don't know. I saw him today before I was taken to the house and he told me what to cut."

Inhaling Jax studied Georgia carefully. "What were you supposed to cut for Mr. Santarino?"

Georgia looked into her eyes, her lips trembling slightly. "He want twenty, two-carat diamonds cut from the big diamond."

"How many did you get cut?"

"Only four."

"Okay, that would leave a diamond of around 154.5 carats. What is he going to do with that?"

She shook her head as if to say she didn't know and Jax wasn't falling for it. "Do not tell us you don't know."

Another tear tracked down Georgia's cheek before she quietly said, "Miss Crowe hide it for a while in her barn with the others. Then he call me to come back and cut more next year."

Her comm chirped, "Fuck Little Mama, we were right there."

Tapping her unit, she replied. "Yeah. But that is a big damned place."

Georgia offered. "She keeps the jewels by the horses in a false wall."

Swinging her head to look at Georgia she saw her shrug as much as she could with her arms behind her back.

"How do you know that Georgia?"

"I have to go there sometimes to take the cut jewels there. Mr. Santarino don't like to come here. He pay me to cut the jewels and store them in the proper way so they don't get lost."

Jax's mind whirled with information. They needed to find Mangus yet. Where in the hell could he be? "Where does he stay when he's in town, Georgia?"

"I don't know. I promise I would tell you. I just want to go home. Not jail."

Ford turned in his seat. "We need to take Georgia to the barn and she needs to show us where the false wall is."

Georgia stared at him, recoiling back slightly. Ford's dark eyes could look rather daunting if he was in the right mood. Like now. All irritated and such.

Smoothing things over, or trying to, she touched Georgia's shoulder again. "Georgia, when you go out to the barn, how do you get there?"

Georgia swallowed, glanced at Ford again then quickly back to her. "Mr. Santarino have a man drive me."

"How does that man get onto the property?"

"He show a card to a man."

Josh looked up into the rearview mirror. "Hang on, we're going back to Stan's. We'll check the guard for a security ID card. Ford, call Hawk and Axel."

30

A TROVE OF STOLEN JEWELS

J ax ran up to Dodge's room and knocked on the door. The door opened and the smile that greeted her was a sight. She stepped into his arm, careful not to jostle his injured one, and wrapped her arms around his waist. Tilting her head back to look up at him she was surprised by the kiss that he planted on her lips. It was brief, too brief, but she'd take it.

"We got it. Most of it. We got it."

"Great job. How much of it is left?"

"Around 154.5 carats."

"Okay, still a huge chunk left."

"Yeah." She backed up a step. "I need the keys to the rental."

He walked to the television stand and picked up the keys. "Ford parked it out back. Be careful, Little Mama."

"Why do you call me that?"

"I don't know. When I first saw you, the first thing that came to my mind was, 'Whoa little mama.' That's still what I think when I see you."

She smiled. That's a good answer. "You've just made me speechless. Don't get used to it though."

Taking the keys she stood up on her toes and touched her lips to his once more. "Gotta go, they're waiting."

"Keep your head down, Little Mama."

"Will do." She responded over her shoulder as she closed the door behind her. Her heart felt light and happy for the first time in...well in forever.

Deciding to take the stairs she spent some of her new energy running down the three flights to the ground level. She tapped her comm unit, "Got the keys, it's out back, see you there."

Stepping out the door she looked across the parking lot and spotted the rental. Jogging to it, she saw the Beast come around the corner of the hotel as she unlocked the car. The Beast stopped in front of her and she opened the backdoor on the driver's side and helped Georgia step down. Her hands were still bound behind her, and she wasn't going to untie her just yet.

Ford jumped out of the Beast and opened the rental's front passenger door, waiting for Georgia to get in. He cut the zip tie binding her hands, and then retied them with a new zip tie in front of her. Looking up he said, "Jax, grab a jacket or something to cover her hands."

Running to the back of the Beast, she pulled one of her hoodies from her bag and the empty box she'd originally had the pink diamond and its cut stones in. She'd moved the diamond and the stones to the console in the Beast, where they were sure to be safe. Climbing into the backseat of the rental, she tapped Georgia's seat twice letting Ford know she was ready to go. He secured the seatbelt around Georgia and closed the door. Ford got into the driver's seat and she reached forward with the keys. He wasted no time getting them on the road.

She knew the plan, Josh would follow them with the Beast and when they turned up the driveway to Mags's place, he'd drive around and enter the property through the trail Wyatt had found earlier today, only he'd breach the fence and come in from the back of the barn so they had the Beast close by.

The drive was largely silent. Only one comment came in over their comm units. Gaige reported, "Local PD left Mags's a half hour ago, she's not there, not sure where she is. Comm units are now live."

That was good news, Mags wouldn't have enough time to move anything. But they didn't know if she'd found her boy's dead body in the vacant store or the one out at Stan's. Surely she knew about the ones in the barn.

Georgia sniffed as she shed a few tears and Jax wondered if she was scared of seeing Mags and lying to her or if she was lying to them and scared they'd kill her if they found out. She'd already knew her guards were shot by Josh, so she had reason to be scared.

Ford said, "Half mile, Jax."

Reaching over the seat, she lay her hoodie over Georgia's bound hands and lay the box on the console between Ford and Georgia. She then pulled the backseat down, crawled through to the trunk and pulled the seat up. Hopefully, they wouldn't check the trunk. But she'd be ready if they did. Pulling a gun from her ankle holster, she clicked a bullet into the chamber and held it up, pointing at the back of the trunk in case they opened it.

She felt the car slow and turn and knew they were rolling up the driveway. She inhaled a large breath and let it out slowly.

The car slowed to a stop. She listened in the dark for any movement or sound. The guard asked, "ID?"

Ford held up the ID card they'd found on the dead guard and she saw a flashlight shine into the backseat between the gap in the seat backs. Bracing herself the guard snapped. "Trunk!"

Hearing his footsteps on the gravel outside, she had her gun raised and ready. Ford popped the lid and the instant the guard's face came into view she shot him three times. She heard Ford's weapon fire and peered around for more guards.

Ford yelled, "Clear." And the car lurched forward. Bracing herself with her feet on the back of the trunk so she wouldn't fly out, she waited until the car evened out, holstered her pistol, then pushed the seat down and climbed through. Just as she'd righted herself, he pulled up to the barn and slowed down. Waiting for anyone to come busting out of the barn shooting. No one did.

Relaying the information, she said, "Josh, we're at the front of the barn. We had to kill two guards at the house. Not sure what's waiting for us inside. How far away are you? Out."

"Just went through the fence and should be coming over the hill in three seconds. Out."

Ford drove around the barn, and she watched for any movement. Reaching the back of the barn, he turned the car facing out and she quickly scrambled out of the trunk. Opening the passenger door, she reached in and unbuckled Georgia's seatbelt, then taking her upper arm, she helped her from the car. She was shaking and crying and honestly, Jax felt sorry for her.

"Georgia, be quiet. If someone is in there, they'll come out shooting."

Quickly ushering Georgia to the side of the barn, she once again pulled her gun from her ankle holster and held it up in front of her, but Georgia whimpered. "I'm telling you this, if you cause them to come out, I'm pushing you forward and I'll protect myself with your body. Serious as hell, Georgia."

Georgia smartly stopped whimpering and nodded her head. Josh pulled up to the barn and jumped from the Beast, stealthily making his way to the barn. She nodded to him and he and Ford entered the barn first. This was the same door she and Dodge had entered earlier today. Since it was dark out, her eyes didn't need time to adjust, she edged Georgia along the wall. Ford and Josh moved through the barn ahead of them, Josh whispering in his comm. "All clear to the apron."

Moving them forward from the wall to the apron of the barn, in between stacks of hay, she maneuvered Georgia in front of her.

Ford whispered, "In front of the horse section."

Light poured into the barn when the door opened and Georgia gasped as the blood on the floor of the apron became visible. Shaking her head, "We killed four men here today. Shut up or there'll be more."

Pushing Georgia to the door of the horse stable, she waited a beat until Josh said, "All clear."

She and Georgia entered the stable area. "Show me the false wall, Georgia."

Georgia hesitated a moment then asked, "I show you and you get me home, yes?"

"We'll get you home after you show us the false wall and how to get into it AND we find Mr. Santarino and put him out of business."

Josh grew impatient. "Let's get moving; we may not have a lot of time."

Georgia's voice quivered slightly when she responded. "It is over here."

Still holding her upper arm Jax followed Georgia as she led them to a small office area and pulled a chair away from the wall. Stopping, Georgia turned to lock eyes with her. "Go ahead, Georgia, open the wall and hurry."

Georgia reached up into a cabinet hanging on the wall. Josh warned, "Careful and slow, Georgia."

Her eyes flicked to Josh then back to the cabinet. Pushing a button at the back, a panel opened in the wall next to the cabinet. Jax pulled Georgia back and Ford stepped in and opened the wall. Narrow shelves lined the opening and small boxes rested on the shelves. Some of them were dusty, others not. Josh pulled on a pair of rubber gloves he had tucked in his pocket and picked up one of the boxes. A large sapphire rested in cotton. He held it out to Ford but said, "Lincoln, didn't you say Lynyrd Station PD told you of a sapphire that had gone missing?"

"Yes, a 64-carat sapphire that they suspected Mangus had stolen."

Looking at Georgia, Josh asked, "Is this around 64-carats?"

Squaring her shoulders, she looked into his brown eyes and proudly said, "It is approximately 52.6 carats now."

Josh replaced the lid and opened another box revealing emeralds. He turned to look at Georgia then said, "Gaige, you better call your contact with the feds. I think we have a treasure trove of stolen jewels here."

31

FOR ADAM

The door opened and he turned from the window to see Jax, looking radiant even though she wore black. Jeans, long sleeve t-shirt, boots, all of it was black. Her hair, which she almost always wore in a ponytail was pulled back. But it was her smile that lit up the room. It was gorgeous. She was gorgeous. Walking toward him she giggled.

"We scored big."

Holding his right arm out, his heart hammered when she walked to him, her arms wrapping around his waist, his right arm pulling her close, even though his left arm was in a sling between them. He inhaled the scent of her hair and reveled in her warmth.

"Great job, Little Mama."

He kissed the top of her head and lay his cheek on the place he'd just kissed. She moved and he lifted his head to look into her eyes but her lips captured his in an instant and he loved the way that felt even more.

Her tongue dipped into his mouth and danced along his. His right hand cupped her nape, just under her ponytail and held her mouth to his and his lips mated with hers. She stepped back then, but stayed close. "We've only got a few minutes before Wyatt will be back and chances are Ford and Josh will come in as well so we can debrief the team back home."

She took his right hand and led him to his bed, sitting and patting the space beside her. "I may have let Josh think we're an item. I don't think there is an issue with it, but I just wanted to give you a heads up. When he asked if we were together, I told him it was none of his business and that he needed to back off. I didn't clarify anything further. I..."

He placed his forefinger over her lips, his eyes sought hers. "Don't worry about it. I rather like the idea of us being together. At least of us thinking about trying out dating."

Her eyes widened and her smile grew. He removed his finger, dipped his head down, and kissed her lips briefly. "What do you think?

"If it doesn't work out, it may be awkward for a while."

"Then I'll take every assignment that takes me out of town."

She giggled, "You shouldn't have to do that."

"How about we don't borrow trouble and see where this goes?"

The door opened and Wyatt stepped in. "Interrupting?"

"No." Jax snapped.

Josh and Ford walked in behind him and other than a brief glance at their closeness, no one said anything else. Wyatt began hooking up cords from his laptop to the television in the room so they could see their remote team as they debriefed. He pulled up their software and then connected them to GHOST headquarters back at Lynyrd Station.

The screen blipped a few times then the rest of their team came into view. She scooted Dodge back to rest against the headboard, then sat next to him. Ford sat at the foot of the bed, Josh and Wyatt perched themselves at the foot of the other bed so they could all be seen.

Gaige started. "Hi everyone and great job."

Gaige and Lincoln congratulated them on a job well done then Gaige got to business. "Okay, debrief. What do you have for a diamond?"

Jax sat up straighter and replied. "Georgia had cut four, two-carat pieces from the stone which leaves approximately 154.5 carats left. Still one of the largest rough pink diamonds in the world and, hopefully, Guardwell will be happy with that much and the four smaller stones."

Gaige nodded then looked at him. "Dodge, how are you doing?"

He cleared his throat. "I'm fine. The pain has lessened and in a couple of days, I'll be just fine."

"Okay. Sorry to start your first mission out this way. But, baptism by fire and all."

He chuckled, that's for sure. He asked in return, "Any sightings of Mangus?"

Lincoln spoke up then. "As a matter of fact, yes. We got word late last night that he was spotted in a little town about 80 miles from Jasperville. He turned around and began driving back here. We're guessing someone got word to him of the shit-show happening. We set up cameras in the area and we know how he gets in and out now. We have him on camera entering his mountain hideout. We're going out there the morning once Hawk and Axel return to see if we can get him. We're assuming he's tucking in now that some of the shit is going down."

Jax smiled and locked eyes with him and his heart fluttered. Like a fucking teenage girl his stomach twisted and his heart thumped along like it was in a race. "Isn't that fantastic?" She asked and all he could do was smile in return and nod.

"Okay, so tomorrow you should be able to come home. The feds will deal with Mags and I'll report in as soon as I hear from our contact."

Lincoln smiled and looked at him. "For Adam." Gave him a thumbs up and dammit if it didn't bring tears to his eyes. Ford tapped him on the leg then. "For Adam. He'd be so proud."

Swallowing the gigantic lump in his throat all he could do was nod. Jax lay her head against his chest and snaked an arm around his waist. Gaige looked at them, his brows rose but to his credit, he said nothing. They'd no doubt have a discussion when they all got back to HQ. But for now, this was a moment he'd never forget.

32

THIS IS GONNA BE FUN

Waking, Jax stood from her bed and walked to the bathroom to shower and go see how Dodge was doing this morning. Her room connected to his and Wyatt's and she'd tossed and turned all night thinking of him being just a room away. Her head spun at the thought of actually dating. They hadn't even had sex yet, they hadn't spent any time not being on a mission or co-workers so that was something they'd have to do. As soon as they got back home, maybe they'd go out to eat and talk. Then, maybe more than talk.

Her nipples pebbled at the thought. Then wetness gathered between her legs and she ducked under the running water to cool herself off.

Working through her routine she silently prayed for three things: The feds would locate the jewels and other incriminating evidence to get Mags; Gaige and the rest of the team would get Mangus even though she wasn't there; and that Stan would be alright.

Blow drying her hair she allowed her thoughts to stray again to Dodge and what she thought about him as a person. The little that she knew was that he was smart. He'd also suffered loss. He was a good cop, a great teammate, and he was incredibly sexy. Also, he genuinely seemed like a good guy. She hoped he'd see the tree she and Josh had planted for Jake as a loving tribute and not something stupid, 'cause that might be a deal breaker.

Her phone rang as she hung the dryer back on the wall and she scooted to pick it up. Dodge's picture popped up on her screen and a smile grew across her face. Tapping the answer icon she said, "Good morning. How are you feeling today?"

"Morning. Sore. But good."

"I don't think sore and good are the same thing. Actually kind of the opposite."

"Well, I meant, I'm sore. But the pain has lessened and I don't feel light-headed anymore. So, good."

She laughed at his explanation. "Okay. That's fair."

"Are you ready to go down for breakfast? We're eating at the hotel restaurant."

"Yep, just give me five minutes to put some clothes on and I'll be in."

"Fuck, Little Mama, don't put clothes on for me."

"Shut up." She giggled as she hung up and began pulling her clothes from her duffle.

Quickly dressing in her jeans, she topped them off with a dark blue cami and a blue and black plaid shirt, left unbuttoned. Sliding her feet in tall, black leather boots she felt sexy and ready for whatever the day brought. Quickly she packed the rest of her items in her duffle and gathered her bathroom supplies and dried them. She tossed them in the side pocket of her duffle. She'd drop it in the Beast before breakfast. Bending at the waist she gathered her hair up into a ponytail, secured it with an elastic tie. She stood, glanced in the mirror, grabbed her bag and tossed it over her shoulder before she knocked on the door that connected her room to Dodge and Wyatt's, but mostly her thoughts were on Dodge. Again.

The door opened and a few things hit her all at once. The scent from Dodge fresh from the shower was the best scent in the world. His large frame encased in a t-shirt made him the sexiest man on earth, even with his arm in a sling in front of some of his yumminess. And, she could look into those green eyes For. Ever. Or close. But, a long time. Damn.

He bent his knees, leaned in and kissed her and her damned nipples tightened to the point of hurting.

He inhaled then whispered, "Best aroma in the world right here. You smell amazing, Little Mama."

Speechless. He left her speechless. That hardly ever happened. Look what this man was doing to her. Her mind wandered constantly to doing bad things with him, to what he thought, to what he smelled like, and Gawd, she was like a teenager again.

"Let's go lovebirds, I'm starving." Wyatt appeared out of the bathroom, looking fresh and ready to attack the day.

Dodge stepped back and chuckled and she entered their room, her cheeks flaming a bright red, if the heat was an indicator. Dodge walked to his bed and grabbed the duffle on the end of it and slung it over his right shoulder.

"I can take..." She started but the look on his face stopped her.

"I'm not an invalid, Little Mama. And I'm not going to have a woman carrying my bag for me."

Her brows rose and her lips tightened. But he continued. "I'm also not letting a man carry my bag for me so before you start in on your Tarzan bullshit, note that and pack it away."

Wyatt laughed and grabbed his bag. "I think you two are going to do just fine." He tossed his bag over his shoulder as he opened the door and stepped out.

Dodge waited for her to proceed him and she hesitated for a millisecond, then decided she sort of liked that he treated her with chivalry, so she stepped out the door behind Wyatt without another word.

Waiting at the elevator Josh and Ford met them and the five piled into the elevator with minimal conversation other than the two asking Dodge how he felt this morning.

They exited the elevator without a word, walked out the lobby door amid stares and open mouths of some of the women. Jax had to admit it made her feel pretty damned good that she was with this good looking group and all the women were jealous of her position. If they only knew what the group did for a living.

Depositing their bags in the Beast they went back inside and were seated at a table toward the back of the restaurant, which suited them just fine. Breakfast conversation was limited to personal things and just as their breakfasts were served Josh said, "I'm only going to say this once, but I want to say it in front of everyone." He looked directly at Dodge and continued. "If you hurt my sister, I'll kill you."

Dodge grinned. "Will you kill her if she hurts me?"

Josh was speechless and made her chuckle even though she could feel her cheeks brighten again. "Don't be an asshole."

Dodge laughed then and so did Wyatt. Ford took a

drink of his coffee and looked Jax in the eye. "I'll kill you if you intentionally hurt Dodge. Just so things are even."

Josh froze mid-chew and glared across the table at Ford. Ford simply nodded then began attacking his food.

Wyatt chuckled again and swallowed his mouthful before lightening the mood. "This is gonna be fun."

33

FOR JAKE

They loaded up in the Beast and called in to headquarters.

Gaige answered. "Morning team are you ready for today?"

After they'd all answered he continued on. "I spoke to my contact at the State Department. The feds have Mags. They found her leaving town and guess where she was headed? Right here to Lynyrd Station. So, we're going out this morning, the four of us, to break into Mangus' hideout. Report in when you get back. And, Georgia is still in Stangleville jail. She's bitching that you all lied to her and she wants to go home. I have a feeler out to the local Koevoet in her hometown in South Africa. I'm checking to see if she's a criminal there or if there are any outstanding warrants for her. I'll let you know when I hear something. Out."

The screen went black. Dodge and Jax climbed out of the Beast to return the rental. She jumped into the driver's seat before he got to the car. He stopped and looked at her through the window but all she did was smile back at him and point to the passenger side.

Damned woman. But she did make things interesting.

Climbing into the passenger side, he struggled getting the seat belt pulled around his arm. She snorted, then took control. "Let me help you, Tarzan."

Liking her assistance he held still as she buckled his seat belt, then cupped her cheek with his right hand. "I love that you want to help me."

Her eyes. Her gorgeous, brown, sparkly eyes looked deeply into his. Her soft lips curved into a serene smile. Bending forward he touched his lips to hers and his heartbeat sped up when she moved her lips with his. Her tongue slipped between his lips and slid along his tongue in the most sensual way. She pulled back slightly, nipped at his bottom lip, and he heard her inhale deeply.

The Beast's horn blew and quick as a rabbit she flipped them off while starting the rental. He laughed out loud and she followed suit. Ducking his head he looked up at Ford, who sat in the passenger seat and his grin said it all.

After returning the rental, they climbed in the backseat of the Beast and started for home. He hadn't taken any pain pills today and his head felt clear. He actually felt pretty good, except a dull throbbing where the incision was. And, maybe a little tugging where the bullet went in, but he was tough, he could handle it. But, they had a six-hour drive ahead of them, so he thought maybe he'd nap on the way.

***

He woke with his cheek pressed to the top of Jax's head. Her head lay on his right shoulder. It was cozy. Wyatt sat on the other side of Jax, snoring semi-quietly and the temperature in the truck was warm. Lifting his head, Josh glanced into the rearview and nodded to him. Ford looked back and smiled. "Have a nice nap?"

"I did. I guess I'm not one hundred percent yet."

"What're their excuses?" Ford nodded to Jax and Wyatt. He chuckled. "Good point."

The computer screen lit up and Ford pushed the button to answer the call from headquarters. Gaige's voice sounded over the computer, but no picture. "How far out are you? We're in trouble here."

Jax and Wyatt both sat up all of them staring at the computer as if the answers would appear. Josh responded, "We're ten miles out. Where are you and what's the problem?"

"Hawk's been shot, he's alive but down. Axel and Lincoln are holding their position at the entrance of Mangus' hideout in the mountain. We intercepted him going out, engaged in fire and his men returned fire. They came out of nowhere, like ants leaving a burning hill. I don't want to let the son of a bitch back inside. Out."

"We'll be right there."

Josh stepped on the gas and Jax turned and began pulling weapons from the back of the Beast. They each had their assault rifles. Jax loaded Josh's rifle and one for Dodge. The clicking and closing of weapons being loaded and checked was all that could be heard in the SUV. That and the tires chewing up the road. Tossing flak jackets up to the guys she said to Dodge, "I'll help you get this on so you don't get a matching hole in your body."

Slowly he began pulling his sling off his shoulder, the Velcro straps sounded loud in the SUV. Wyatt and Ford shrugged their jackets on and Jax did the same. He'd be lying if he said he wasn't a bit creeped out now. A little

PTSD after just being shot yesterday was understandable, but he needed to shake that shit off. As if he could read thoughts, Ford looked back at him. "You okay?"

"Yeah."

Ford nodded. "For Adam."

"For Adam." He whispered back.

Josh looked at him in the rearview mirror. "Dodge, I'm not saying you can't do this, but let's be smart. I'll let everyone out of the Beast just before we get there, they can run in unseen. I'll turn the Beast around and back in, wedging Mangus in. You need to be in the back and when you have a good shot, you need to take it. You good with that?"

He swallowed some of his pride, no matter how you looked at it, but he'd do what was needed. And, hopefully, he'd finish Mangus off before he hurt anyone else. "Yeah. I'm good."

Josh tapped the computer. "We're coming in, three on foot and two in the Beast."

"Come up the drive and don't waste any time." Gaige yelled. Gunshots could be heard in the background and the dire situation became real.

Jax climbed back over the last seat and sat down, then helped him climb over without reinjuring his shoulder. The movement made him break out in a sweat, and he took in several deep breaths before scooting to the back window and pulling his gun up ready to shoot.

Jax called out to him, "Hey."

He turned to look at her. "For Adam." Her brows raised as she locked eyes with him.

His voice cracked when he replied. "For Adam."

Josh called out, comm on live. He stopped the vehicle and Ford, Wyatt and Jax climbed out and scrambled off into the trees and shrubbery surrounding Ryker Mountain. Once they were out of sight Josh looked back at him. "Showtime."

Nodding he turned to the back of the Beast, lifted his rifle and took a deep breath. Just as they turned a corner, Mangus' red Buick came into view. The driver's door was open and it looked empty. Just before they reached the car, Mangus came running from a grouping of bushes and jumped into his car. Josh yelled, "Brace."

Dodge had just enough time to but both feet up on the hatch door to keep from flying through the window. The impact was enough to do damage to Mangus' car so he couldn't drive it, but not enough to hurt him. Perhaps only dazed and confused. He looked through the window as Mangus looked up, shook his head, then pierced him with his evil eyes. The moment it dawned on Mangus that he'd seen Dodge before, his eyes got round and he raised his gun to shoot. Tapping the button to lower the back window with his foot, Dodge let out a hail of bullets, to rival a World War II movie. The holes left in Mangus' car were too many to count without marking them. But, mostly what he saw was the blood on the windshield from blowback, and Mangus' head resting against the seat back, two red holes in his head. "Gotcha, motherfucker."

A few more gunshots rang out, Josh shot a couple rounds from the front of the Beast, then silence fell on the mountain.

He and Josh waited in the Beast until they saw Ford and Lincoln walking toward him. Lifting the hatch with the second button in the back, Dodge slowly scooted himself from the back of the vehicle, laying his rifle just inside in case he needed to use it again.

"It's all good, buddy." Lincoln said. Then his friend embraced him. "You okay?"

"Yeah. Been a hell of a start but I've gotta say, I think I like this."

Both of his friends laughed. "Yeah, it's pretty fucking amazing." Ford responded.

Jax and Wyatt came out of the brush and walked toward him, vigilant in case a rouge gunman still remained. Her eyes locked with his then turned to Mangus. Walking to the driver's door, she looked inside and stood silent for a long moment. He quietly approached her and stood next to her, allowing her the time she needed. Turning to him she softly said, "Thank you."

He nodded and replied, "For Jake."

Tears sprang to her eyes and her lip trembled. His first reaction was 'fuck no' he hated when women cried. But, he held his right arm out for her to walk into his embrace and when she did, he just stood there and held her until she was ready to move.

Josh came over and looked into the car, patted his sister on the back then joined their teammates.

Allowing Jax the time she needed, he stood with her silently. She didn't dwell on this for a long while, whatever she told herself in her thoughts, she quickly said it, straightened and sniffed. "Let's get your sling back on Tarzan. Hate to have you hurt yourself again."

Three hours later, they left the hospital after ensuring Hawk would be okay. He was shot in the left side, and luckily, no major organs were injured. He'd be spending the night for sure, maybe two. Lynyrd Station PD had released them all to go home, and they'd spend the remainder of the night investigating, writing up their reports, etc. It didn't mean they wouldn't be questioned again, but for the most part, it was clear what GHOST did and Lynyrd Station PD was happy as were the feds. Their contact at the State Department already had things rolling to make sure GHOST didn't feel any heat on this one.

34

SOUNDS LIKE A WIN/WIN

The Beast pulled into the garage at headquarters. She sighed to see home again but she didn't plan on staying. Not tonight anyway.

Their team climbed from the vehicle each of them with a sigh and maybe a groan or two. It had been a full couple of days. Pulling their bags from the back of the Beast, Gaige and the second team unloaded from the second Beast, which they still needed to name, and said, "Let's debrief tomorrow at 08:00 hours. Sleep good everyone."

Various good nights were called out and Josh, Wyatt, and Axel headed to the elevator while Ford and Lincoln headed to their trucks. She turned to Dodge and said, "I want to come home with you."

His smile was beautiful. Perfect really. "That right?"

"Yes. I'm one hundred percent positive that I want to spend the night with you. I'll help you take care of your arm, wrap it up for your shower, and well, that's good, right?"

"Little Mama, you don't see me arguing do you?"

She giggled. She'd been afraid he'd say no. "I'll drive."

"You want to drive my truck?"

"I do."

"Shit, Little Mama."

She tossed her bag into the backseat, closed the door, then opened the driver's door and jumped in. Reaching her hand out for the keys, she smiled at his reluctance, but he only seemed to be toying with her more than being reticent to comply. Pulling the keys from his front pocket, he handed them over to her, walked around the front of the truck, climbed in the passenger door, and closed it. "Let's head home."

She snickered again, put the truck in reverse and backed out of his parking spot. The garage door slid open as the truck neared and she eased the big vehicle from the garage. At the end of the driveway she stopped and looked at him. "Which way, Tarzan?"

"Take a right and head out of town. I'm at the bottom of Lynyrd Station on the Hill."

"Isn't that Ford's mountain?"

"Yep." He chuckled. "Lincoln and I live at the bottom of the mountain on opposite sides of the river."

"Handy."

"By design. We wanted to be close but not too close. Ford had the land, we each bought our lots and proceeded to build. Lincoln's is finished. Mine, well there's still decorating to do. It's not my thing."

Shaking her head she said, "Me either. And, I don't cook or clean and I'm only a mediocre nurse."

She braved a glance in his direction and saw him smiling. "But you shoot like a demon, you run into situations where guns are blazing to help a teammate. You're smart, sexy, and kind of fun to be around. And Megan's a nurse, so there's that."

She looked at him again, back to the road and to Dodge again. No one had ever said things like that about her. No one.

Then her face scrunched. "Really?"

He burst out laughing and she gripped the steering wheel tightly. Stupid to be jealous, but dammit, that little jealousy bug bit her anyway.

"Megan is sexy as fuck. Long, auburn hair, voluptuous body, stubborn as a mule, and a nurse. Remember, she's also Ford's wife and the mother of his daughter?"

Rolling her eyes, she raised her right hand to punch him in the arm and he reared back so fast she thought he'd fly out of the truck. Realizing she would have hit his injured arm she dropped her hand. "Sorry." Then she burst out laughing. "But you should see your face."

"Turn right up at the driveway."

Slowing his truck she navigated the driveway and turned the bright headlights on to see. The world was dark out here at the base of the mountain. Dark and serene.

"Stay right up here."

Following directions he pointed to a turn to the left. "That's Lincoln and Skye's driveway."

"Oh, wow."

It was pitch black up Dodge's driveway and once again she wondered if she ever had the chance, would she want Skye to tell her about Jake's death. Josh's words came back to her and she shook her head to rid herself of the thoughts.

"He's already home and they're probably already in

bed." His grin was adorable. His eyes skated to hers. "They're newlyweds."

Nodding to continue to watch the narrow drive they were on as it curved them to the left and around the mountain. The road shifted uphill briefly then back down.

"We just drove over the river. Isn't that cool?"

She wanted to turn and see it again. "Maybe tomorrow when it's light you can show it to me."

"Sure thing."

He fidgeted with an invisible piece of lint on his trousers and she wondered what was suddenly wrong. He'd seemed fine with her coming home with him, but the closer they got, the quieter he became.

"You may as well tell me what's going on in your head, Tarzan. We're going to be together for a while."

He sat up straighter and cleared his throat. "How do you feel about me killing Mangus?"

"I feel fine. I wanted to be the one to do it. I've dreamed about it. Making him pay for Jake's death. I know it was mostly Victor, but those two together were like a hell on this earth. There was nothing they did that was upstanding or right. They stole, lied, cheated, killed, dealt in death and destruction. There was nothing they did that should keep them alive."

He nodded. "I had the feeling you planned to kill him. Truth be told, it was one of the reasons I killed him. Not to take it away from you, but to keep you from doing something that you might one day regret. Not that you would, but this way you have a clear conscience."

"I hope you do as well."

"I do. Sometimes that makes me feel like I'm a bad person."

Reaching over to touch his thigh, she replied. "You are not a bad person."

"For the most part I'm not. But, in our line of work we do bad things: killing all those guys in the barn, even though they would have killed us first and they've probably killed others for Mags or Mangus. But, I try to remember that taking out the garbage isn't glamorous or even something anyone wants to do, but it needs to be done or the house stinks."

"Yep. That's right. My father taught me that a long time ago. I was just a little girl when he began working for GHOST. Back then, Gaige's father ran things. Now it's him and both of our fathers are gone. But, my dad believed in what GHOST was doing. He loved it. So did Jake and so does Josh. I do, too. I don't always like the situations we're in, but I love at the end of the day knowing I took the garbage out."

Suddenly lights lit up and illuminated the driveway, which then curved first left then right, then stopped at an impressive house. Putting the truck in Park, she turned to look at Dodge. "Welcome home."

He chuckled, "I should be saying that to you."

He opened his door and stepped out of the truck, which considering he was in a sling, he made look graceful as if he always did it. Pulling his bag from the backseat he slung it over his good shoulder, and waited for her in front of the truck.

Stepping up next to him, he chuckled but began moving toward the house. "Lincoln's sister, Josie, is a big time interior designer. She's offered to decorate for me and I hadn't taken her up on it before she got some big ass fancy hotel design job. She's almost finished with it, so I think I'll have her come up here and decorate away. How do you feel about that?"

"Did you ever sleep with her?"

He laughed. "No. She's a bit too bossy for me. Plus she's married and has kids."

"Then I think it's a great idea."

"It'll make Skye happy too, they can spend some time together."

"Sounds like a win/win."

35

YOU'RE A SEXY WOMAN

Since she'd told him about Hawk and her, he'd had some doubts. Then he thought about how they'd acted at breakfast a few days ago, as if nothing had ever happened and he'd felt better. Then he swore at himself for acting like a stupid grade schooler with his first crush.

Opening the front door, he stood back and let her enter before him. She snickered and walked past him. Once inside, the lights clicked on and she set her bag on the floor alongside the sofa and looked around. The overly large fireplace he had in the middle of the far wall was certainly the focal point and masterpiece in the room. Good thing 'cause there was little else in it.

He'd used a large 8 x 8 beam from a barn back home for the mantle and stone he'd picked from the river in his backyard.

"Wow, that's impressive."

"Pieces of home and pieces of here." He replied as he pointed to the mantle and the rocks. "It works and makes me think it's meant to be."

"That's pretty nice."

He tossed his keys on a table next to the door and walked into the kitchen, which was open to the living room. "Anyway, not sure if you want to shower, I know I do. And, since you don't cook, I can toss a casserole into the oven that Megan made for me. That way we can eat."

"She's your nurse and she cooks for you?"

Chuckling he turned and looked into her eyes. Even a few feet away he could see the clarity in them. There was a pull between them, an unexplainable pull and even if he lived to be a thousand years old, he'd never be able to explain it.

"She and Skye both feel sorry for me. When they make big meals, they make extra and freeze it. Every so often I'm gifted with casseroles, lasagnas, baked breads, and cookies. Little do they know that I can cook, but I'm keeping that a secret." He winked and a smile grew across her gorgeous face.

"That's lying by omission."

"I suppose." He stood in place as she slowly walked toward him. "You gonna tell?"

She laughed. "Well, if we enjoy spending time with each other, that would be stupid. I've told you I don't cook. That's not even a little lie. I. Do. Not. Cook. Ever. Good thing you can."

He reached out with is right hand and cupped the back of her head, pulling her closer to him. Staring into her eyes he saw so much in them. His heart pounded in his chest like a prisoner trying to get out and his cock grew and thickened as he struggled with which one to pay attention to more. Inhaling her scent, she still smelled fresh and clean even after running through gunpowder and the woods. Crazy.

Bending his head he kissed her lips, slow, soft, moving his lips over hers the temperature in the room rose and his skin dampened, every time a sigh or a moan escaped from her. Her hands grabbed his shirt on both sides and if it weren't for his damned lame arm between them, he'd love nothing more than to feel her breasts tight against his chest.

Tilting his head he fit his lips over hers and deepened the kiss. The taste of her tongue was sweet, the warmth felt like home and the softness like a feather bed.

She pulled back and all he felt was loss. "I would like to jump in the shower if you don't mind."

Her cheeks were flushed but it only enhanced her beauty. She wasn't a sweet innocent by any stretch of the imagination, but what she was, was perfect for him. Tough, resilient, strong and yet a woman that he hoped would be in his life for a longtime.

Clearing his throat, he said, "Absolutely, follow me."

Walking through the kitchen, she grabbed her bag as they entered the living room and he led her down a short hallway past two doorways which were a spare bedroom and his office. Then, he turned and flipped on the light to his bedroom, and stepped aside as she entered before him.

"Again, no decorations but at least I have blinds, though there's no one out here." He stepped into the room and passed her to turn on the bathroom light. "But I do have an amazing bathroom."

He watched as she took everything in. The masculine brown marbled tiles on the walls and in the shower, the over-sized shower heads and shower with the glass door. Wooden benches made from the same 8 x 8 beams he'd used for the mantle were both rich and handsome in this room.

She gasped. "This is fantastic."

"Thanks." He was proud of this part of his house. He was proud of the whole house, but this was the room he enjoyed.

Running her hand along the tiles on the walls, he watched her eyes as they lit up with delight. Her fingers ran over the long counter that held two copper sinks.

Stopping to look at him, the smile on her face was hard to decipher but the word pleased came to mind. He cleared his throat. "I'll go throw a casserole into the oven so we can eat."

"Wait." She stopped him from leaving with her hand on his arm. "What do you need to do for your arm to shower?"

"Ahh..." He scraped his right hand through his hair. "I need to keep a bandage over it and not soak it under the spray. Then change it when I get out."

Nodding she replied with a smile. "That I can help with. Show me your first aid kit."

Walking to the large floor to ceiling cabinet along the opposite wall from the shower he opened the top door and pulled down a blue first aid kit. He turned to set it on the counter but she gently took it from his hands. Laying it on the counter she opened it up and looked through the contents as she said over her shoulder. "Take your shirt off and I'll bandage it up with large amount of Vaseline to keep it from becoming saturated and a new bandage."

"What makes you think that is appropriate?"

She turned and locked eyes with him and he swallowed. Slowly stalking toward him she lifted her t-shirt and pulled it off her body. His mouth grew dry and his heartbeat picked up a faster new rhythm. Turning only slightly she pointed to a scar in her side, just above her hip. "I was shot right here ten years ago." Placing her booted foot on the bench alongside him, she untied her laces and quickly took her boot off. Pointing to another scar she said, "Knife wound from an asshole during a mission in California six years ago."

Pulling her other boot off she began unbuttoning her jeans and lowering the zipper. "I have more scars that I can show you, but I'm thinking we should take a shower."

She stepped from her jeans, bent over and picked them up, folded them and lay them on the counter. Doing the same with her t-shirt he took in her body. Flawless olive skin, if you didn't count the scars, lay lovingly over toned muscles all forming a body which he assumed would be stellar, but seeing her in the flesh, pun intended, was more than he'd even thought she would be.

Turning back to him she said, "I'd like to see you to, Tarzan."

Releasing the Velcro on his sling, he gently pulled it off and lay it on the bench next to him. His shirt was a bit more of a struggle as he tried pulling it from his back and over his head. She neared him and gently pulled the neck-line over his head, holding it firmly in place so it didn't jostle his wound. Once his right arm was clear of the offending material, she slowly removed the t-shirt from his left arm.

She folded it, like her own and lay it on top of her clothes and his heart swelled.

"Hold still, Tarzan." It wasn't a demand, but maybe a command? Anyway, who was he not to listen to orders? He stood and she unbuttoned his jeans, lowered the zipper and chuckled a bit as her hand moved over his thickening cock.

Tugging on his waistband, she lowered his jeans to the floor and waited as he stepped from each leg. She repeated the same motions she'd done with their other clothing. Once she stepped before him she lay her hands on his bare chest, careful not to touch the bandage and let her hands smooth over his chest, circling his nipples with her thumbs, then floating down his abs, gently teasing his skin along the waistband of his briefs. He wrestled with wanting to watch her and closing his eyes to enjoy the feel of her hands on him. Her fingers were firm as she touched him, but her hands were surprisingly soft. He'd expected them to be roughened by the way they worked. She was a plethora of surprises. The most surprising right now was the slight tremor he felt in her hands. She didn't strike him as the type to get so excited over sex.

"Tarzan, you're a sexy man." She purred.

Swallowing first he replied. "You're a sexy woman, Little Mama."

36

FASTER

Being a woman working in what is primarily a man's field, Jax had struggled over the years to not become a woman who'd turned into a crass talking, potty-mouthed trailer trash hag. But right now the only words that came to mind were holy fuck. And she meant that kind of literally. Dodge was the total damned package. Sinfully sexy. Smart. Built. Caring. A gentleman. The list went on. And right now, she wanted to be on him like a bee on honey.

Her hands shook slightly as she wrestled between slowly enjoying him and just jumping on him and riding him like a bull. Of course she'd make sure he got his happy ending too, but she really needed her happy ending right now, she'd been thinking about it for a few days.

Taking his hand in hers she tugged him toward the bedroom and to his bed. The king-sized bed stood in the middle of the far wall. Its massive headboard was made of the same wood as the bench in the bathroom and the fireplace mantle. She'd need to ask him later what the wood meant to him. He'd said a little bit from home, but didn't elaborate. Reaching forward she pulled the duvet and sheet back, exposing chocolate colored sheets with a slight sheen to them. She smiled then turned to look up at him.

"Sister-in-law wanted to make sure I had nice sheets before I left home."

"Really? Your brother's wife bought you sheets?"

"Yes. Really. What's wrong with that?"

She shrugged. "It seems kind of weird." Smoothing her hand over the soft silky feeling material she added. "But she has great taste."

He chuckled then tugged his brief's down on the right side. He tried on the left side, but the tugging in his shoulder stopped him and he grimaced.

"Let me help you."

Tugging his underwear down his legs, she took the opportunity to kiss her way up his left leg, swirling her tongue around here and there to delay her ascent. Once she reached his hip, she kissed her way toward his cock then stopped and started at the bottom of his right leg. He let out a groan and she smiled but continued kissing and swirling her tongue on the way up. Reaching his hip, she kissed her way to the center, paused then slowly swiped her tongue from the root to the tip of his cock. His sharp intake of breath told her more than any words could. Sucking him into her mouth she marveled at the satiny feel of his warm skin over the hardness underneath.

In, then out a few times before his hand grabbed her ponytail and fisted it. Adding pressure to the back of her head she fought not to smile but closed her eyes instead and enjoyed listening to his breathing become labored and choppy.

Cupping his balls with her hand, she gently rolled them enjoying the contrast of the springy hairs covering the softness of his sac. He pulled on her ponytail, removing himself from her mouth and tilted her head to look up at him.

"Later." He croaked.

Standing she, shimmied her panties down as he backed onto the bed and lay back. She prowled over to him, then straddled his body, lifting up on her knees to position his cock at her wet entrance.

"Pull your hair band out, Jax, I want to see your hair."

She smiled but did as he asked, finger combing her hair as it fell over her shoulders. He stared at it, taking it in as it lay against her skin, his eyes lovingly caressed it. She could almost feel it, his stare was so intense.

"Beautiful." He whispered it and the softness of his voice made her nipples pucker tightly.

"Now the bra. I want to see your tits as you ride me."

That sent a lightning bolt through her body, landing between her legs in a white hot flash. Wetness gathered and her skin flashed red. Reaching behind her back, she unfastened her bra and quickly slid it down her arms, letting it fall to the floor.

"Touch them." Well, damn it, another lightning bolt jolted through her body and she nearly panted. Cupping her breasts for him, she moved them to and fro, rolling her nipples between her thumb and forefinger easing the tension that tightened them to points. Rocking against his cock, she swiped her juices over him, the slippery sensation hitting her in the perfect way.

"Fuck, Little Mama, you're a sexy woman. I could come just watching you get off like that."

Her eyes locked with his and held him in place.

Licking her lips slowly he surprised her by pulling her slightly forward with his right hand, arching his hips up and pushing her back, he pushed himself inside of her. They both let out a low growling moan as their bodies molded to each other and fit together like long lost puzzle pieces.

A wild shiver ran the length of her body and she braced herself with her hands on his chest. He flinched only slightly and she began to pull away, remembering his wound.

"No, don't pull away. Ride."

He didn't have to tell her twice. Slowly she rose and lowered herself on his steel shaft, enjoying the sounds their bodies made together. She closed her eyes and let her body take over. She'd already memorized his body. The way his skin looked with a fine sheen of sweat lovingly caressing the planes and valleys his muscles made. Simply the sexiest man she'd ever met. Mostly because he didn't take her shit, but still respected her. She never dreamed she'd find a man like this.

"Look at me."

Opening her eyes she locked on to his. The green of his irises seemed enhanced in this light, almost as if they glowed and she found it impossible to look away.

"Faster."

Placing both of his hands on her thighs, his left hand not as strong as the right, but still present, he squeezed them as she went faster. Up and down, her body was also coated in a fine sheen and she loved it. She loved this feeling in her heart. He felt right. They felt right somehow.

His left thumb moved over to cover her clit and add

pressure and she panted as he hit that spot. The one. She rose and lowered two more times before she exploded.

His hips rose and fell under her as he sought his release. His breathing was erratic. He let out a loud groan and froze as he pushed himself into her as far as he could. His muscles bunched tightly which felt amazing under her. The light shining in from the bathroom glowed over his skin. Her eyes traveled over his abs then to the bandage at his shoulder, then to where her leg pushed against his side. Their skin tones were different but they looked perfect together.

Slowly lowering herself to lay on him, but not hurt him, her breathing was shallow and raspy, as she tried recover. She smiled as she realized, his chest was heaving from the exertion as well.

Finally he whispered. "Holy fuck."

37

YEP, I'M ON IT

His phone rang in the distance, that nagging constant ringing thumping through his brain. He'd slept the sleep of the dead last night, the best he'd had in days maybe even weeks. Blinking his eyes open his bedroom door came into focus as his brain woke up, and the incessant ringing stopped.

Taking in a deep breath the sweet smell of a woman tickled his nostrils. Jax. Her head lay tucked into his side, just under his arm, which was curved around her shoulders. Her dark hair glistened where the sun streaming through the window touched it. He could see highlights of reds and oranges in the strands, which when mingled together gave off an incredible kaleidoscope of colors, mixed into her mahogany strands.

Her shoulders were bare, so was her back, all the way down to where the sheet rested across her waist, only a peek of ass crack showing. And that was sexy. Memories of loving her last night flooded his brain and his cock jumped to attention in record time, tenting the sheet that lay just over his lower half.

The fucking phone began ringing again and another one in this room. Jax sat up rubbing her eyes then raking her hands through her loose sexy strands. Her eyes locked on his, she smiled, leaned in and kissed his lips then quickly jumped out of bed and walked to her bag in the chair next to the door. Pulling her phone from the side pocket, her nose wrinkled before she tapped the offensive noise box and said, "Yeah."

Her eyes roamed over to his, then down his body in slow perusal and his cock jumped at the look in her eyes. He returned the favor, watching her sexy tits sway as she sauntered toward him like a cat on the prowl. Her legs showed definition in the muscles but not so much that she looked like a body builder, just enough that she looked healthy and alive. The words he first thought when he'd seen her all those days ago, "Whoa, Little Mama", came to the forefront of his mind again.

"Yeah, we'll be there in about a half hour."

Rolling her eyes she snapped, "Would you prefer we meet you there?"

But her hand pulled the sheet down his body, the soft material sliding over his erect cock an unusual sensation which caused pre- come to form on the tip.

"Okay. See you then." Tapping her phone to end the call, she tossed it on the table next to the bed. Her hand slowly reached down and swirled over the pre- come, coating his head with his own juices.

"This right here is sexy, Tarzan." She husked. Her eyes were fixed on her playing as she licked her lips. His cock jumped again and she smiled. "We have to go to work. But first..."

She climbed on the bed, straddling him with her ass facing him. Reverse cowgirl. "Fuck, Little Mama."

"Yep. I'm on it."

His breathing shallowed and if he could get any harder it would be a surprise to him. Raising herself then lowering slowly on his cock, her white hot pussy accepted him fully as she seated herself all the way. Grinding back and forth slowly he could feel the walls of her pussy squeeze his cock and his vision dimmed as little dots formed. Leaning forward, she rested her hands on his ankles, giving him the full view of her sexy round ass and the dark little rosebud which seemed so damned forbidden but yet called to him now. She rocked herself slowly which from this position felt fucking fantastic. Sucking his forefinger into his mouth and pulling out he circled her back entrance twice before slowly easing his finger inside her. She panted on top of him and pushed herself back onto his finger, pushing him in up to his second knuckle. He heard her moan and his balls drew up tight to the point of pain.

Reaching down she rubbed his balls with one hand as she continued to rock on him. "I'm there." She whispered. He pushed his finger into her ass all the way and she gasped as she froze, her body pulsing with her release. He gave her a second, not much more, 'cause he needed to release into her and now. Easing his finger out then back in she began moving faster now, working to get him off and it didn't take more than six strokes. He groaned as his release erupted like hot lava from a volcano. The nagging thought popped into his head that he didn't have a condom on, but the feeling was so beautifully fantastic that he pushed it away.

Jax's head hung over his legs, her back rose and fell with her labored breathing. He couldn't resist moving his finger in and out of her ass to see what her reaction would be. She raised her head back and rocked over him, careful not to lift up so he didn't slip out. He felt semi-erect though it was far too soon for him, but suddenly the thought of getting her off again became more important than anything else.

His left hand held on to her hip as his right hand moved in and out of her sweet tight ass. He saw her move her hand over her clit as she worked herself quickly, her skin flushed to a rosy glow and he worked a second finger into her sweet perfect behind. She gasped at the invasion, but never slowed, her hand moving more furiously at her clit, and fuck that was the hottest thing he'd ever experienced. Fucking Little Mama knew her body and how to use it and he was lost in watching her. She moaned low and long as her orgasm rolled over her, her pussy pulsing over his dick which was a glorious feeling all by itself.

As her pulsing slowed, he slowly removed his fingers and she moaned again. "Fuck, Tarzan." She panted. She pulled herself off of him and rolled smoothly to lay at his side. "Damn," she whispered as her chest moved with her breathing.

"Little Mama, I've said it before, but I'll say it again. You're a fucking queen right here. You make me feel like a teenager. I want to fuck you in every way I can."

She giggled against his chest. "Good 'cause I feel the same way about you."

38

CAN WE TALK LATER?

"He said his contact with the feds called and said something about movement at Mangus' hideout in the mountain entrance and they want us to go and see what we can find out. They have a warrant so that isn't an issue, but they don't have operatives, so we have permission to search the inside.

She navigated the road leading out of the driveway Dodge shared with Lincoln. His truck was smooth as it traveled down the road toward Mangus' hideaway. The longer wheelbase made for a different ride from her Jeep. She still loved her Jeep, but this was nice for a change. Glancing briefly at Dodge, she smiled. "Gaige also said Hawk is up, glaring at nurses and generally being surly."

He chuckled, sat back, relaxed as could be, watching the road ahead of them. A few thoughts traveled through her brain at once. He was relaxed with her driving his truck, something a lot of guys would be uptight about. And, they were about to finish their mission and he seemed as if he'd been doing this for years. Which in some respects he had, but this was a bit different. They didn't need to adhere to search warrants and legal mumbo jumbo, they went in, did their thing, jumped out, and let authorities clean up. It was brilliant.

"I love driving your truck, Tarzan."

He chuckled and her tummy flipped. "Yeah, well I think you need to let me drive your Jeep and see how I like that."

"Deal."

Chuckling again his eyes turned to her. She could see him studying her out of her peripheral vision. She wanted to ask him what he was thinking, but didn't want to sound like a needy teenager. He clued her in soon enough.

"Jax, this thing between us. How do you see it going?"

"What do you mean by that?"

Sitting up straighter he took in a deep breath and warning bells began ringing in her head.

"I mean, do you see this being a long-term relationship? Or, are you having some fun and then you'll move on?"

"How do you see it?"

"I asked you first."

She took a deep breath and tried to quell the nausea that threatened to erupt. Figures he'd be looking to get laid and move on. Why couldn't she see this for what it was? Sexy as fuck, and single at more than 40 years old, she should have guessed he wasn't relationship material. Anger bubbled up her spine, her shoulders tightened, and her back tightened.

"Look, Tarzan, if you're trying to tell me you've had your fun and you're done, just come out and say it. Don't be an asshole and beat around the fucking bush."

"Whoa, whoa, whoa. When did I say that?"

"You're pussyfooting around for some reason."

He shook his head and let out a long, drawn out breath. "Jax." He inhaled. "I'm not pussyfooting and I'm not saying I've had my fun and we're done. Though I did immensely enjoy last night and I'd love to have many, many more like that. This morning too."

His body twisted slightly, his left arm still in the sling, his movements were a bit stilted. He softly added, "Little Mama, we didn't use protection last night or this morning. I just want to know that if you get pregnant you aren't planning on running off."

The air whooshed from her lungs and her mind reeled. Before she could say anything he continued on.

"I've grown to like you. I've grown to look forward to spending time with you. You're sexy, smart, spunky, and incredibly delicious. But, you aren't in a relationship, haven't been married, and I can't help but wonder if that's because you aren't into long-term relationships or what."

She glanced over and locked eyes briefly before looking at the road ahead. "What man wants a woman like me? I live in a man's world. I shoot people, break into homes, I get shot at, I have a dangerous job, and I don't cook. Or clean really."

"I want you."

Tears jumped to her eyes and she had to swallow the gigantic lump that threatened to clog her throat. She couldn't say anything and blinking furiously she slowly pulled the truck to a stop at the edge of the road.

She sat staring straight ahead, both hands gripping the steering wheel as if it were a lifeline. Before she could respond or even think of a response he continued.

"I want you. For all the reasons stated above and more. I share that job with you. I shoot people, break into homes, get shot at, and have a dangerous job. I don't care that you can't cook, I can and we can hire someone to cook for us. Maybe Mrs. James will cook for us and the team. We can hire a housekeeper, maybe Kylie James will clean our house. We know she won't be startled by the dozens if not more weapons laying around. If they can't, we'll find someone else."

She couldn't catch a breath. Her chest heaved as she felt like she was drowning. How many times over the years did she dream of finding someone who was her mirror image in business or work, sexy beyond belief, and had a big heart? Just like her father. Countless was the word that came to mind. The number didn't exist.

Slowly turning her head to look into his eyes, the green irises she couldn't tire of looking at locked onto hers. Sincerity is what she saw beyond the color in them.

A horn blared as a blue Ram truck with a dog's head sticking out the back passenger window sped past them. Lincoln and Abe.

She shook her head and followed the truck, remembering they were on their way to a mission. She quickly responded, "Can we have a nice long talk about this later?"

He turned to face the windshield, and let out a long breath. "Sure."

She could tell those weren't the words he wanted to hear, they needed to have a long conversation and doing it on the way to a mission wasn't the time. But, she'd make sure they had that conversation tonight.

Catching up with Lincoln, she followed him in silence to the meeting point, but her thoughts were a mess. Her dreams were coming true, and she didn't know how to handle it.

39

I'M SORRY TO TELL YOU THIS

Well that didn't go as planned. He was foolish for letting his heart prevail when his head had served him well for many years. Since he'd learned his intoxicated ex-wife was responsible for killing Adam, he'd locked his heart away in a tight little box where it had stayed for fifteen years, safe and sound. Now, this little mama had wormed her way in and unlocked that box without him even realizing it; she was going to break his heart again.

Exiting the truck, he glanced over at Jax as her jaw tightened and she walked toward their team members who had gathered around the back of the Beast for a briefing. Lincoln waited for him at the side of his truck, Abe giving his ear a little lick.

"Everything alright?"

"Yeah."

"Doesn't look like yeah. Dodge this is what Gaige and the rest are worried about. You two having issues affects all of us."

"We're not having issues."

Walking alongside him, Lincoln grunted. "Looks like something is off."

"Yeah. I all but told her I love her and she said we'll talk later."

"You love her?"

"No. I don't know. It's the damnedest thing. There's just this something that I can't let go. A kinship or feeling that a spiritual person would say meant we are destined to be together or something. I don't know what to think about it. I don't know what to do about it. The only thing I know is she feels right for me."

Lincoln laughed out loud and slapped him on the right shoulder. "Well, I'll be damned, you are in love with her."

"I don't know."

They neared their teammates and Gaige started right in explaining their mission. Go in. Investigate. Capture any men left inside. Collect their money. Seemed easy. Their client had strict instructions – no more Santarinos left doing business. Period. Permission to help with the investigation from the feds, helped that along.

"Dodge, how's the shoulder this morning?"

"Good. Pain is minimal, I slept great last night, feeling better."

A few chuckles echoed through the group, but not many as the look on Josh's face sobered the chucklers down.

"Good, so you'll be stationed here on the radio. Stay in the Beast, keep the computers rolling and watch the drone footage and body cams. Ford, Josh and Jax will have cams on. I've got the links already set in the computers."

He handed the body cams out and the team members instantly began putting them on. Gaige finished, "Lincoln and Wyatt you'll be positioned at the back. Body cams go in first and look around, Axel and I will go in next, two paces behind and protect you as you search. Cam team, get in and rush the bums out; immediately begin searching for remaining minions first, documents, stolen property, maps and anything else we can use to shut this operation down. The back team will be ready in case we need backup inside, or if the drones show us another exit point as we're flushing out the criminals."

The group nodded and Dodge's jaw tightened. He hated not being able to go in and help with this. He hated even more that Jax was going in first. Deadly position. His eyes floated to hers and she nodded, gave him a thumbs up, he mouthed "For Jake", she blinked the tears and mouthed, "For Adam." Then adjusted her flak jacket and camera and then she turned and began hiking to the entrance with Ford and Josh.

Climbing into the Beast, his stomach in knots, his back and jaw tight, he positioned himself in the back with the computers. Gaige had them set up in a semi-circle on a shelf built just for this, against the backseat. Both of the computer screens were divided into four squares, to which drone footage, body cams and the two stationary cameras were projected. His teammates voices came over the radio as Jax said, "At the entrance."

Ford and his group replied that they were in position and then Gaige responded the same for his group. Once again Dodge mumbled that sitting on the sidelines was the worst form of torture. That said, sitting on the sidelines while the woman you possibly love was walking into danger was the actual worst form of torture. Note to self - don't get shot and sit on the sidelines again.

The body cams showed on the screens and he couldn't

decide which camera footage to watch - Jax's camera to see what she was seeing or Josh's camera because he was directly behind Jax and he could watch her. His eyes bounced between the two cameras to the point he had the beginnings of a headache. Jax turned to Josh and nodded. Watching her camera, he saw she was at an entrance, a door in front of her. Reaching forward, she checked to see if it was locked. Nodding to Josh, he moved forward and rolled the ACE or Advanced Cutting Explosive, along the frame of the door. Jax moved back, but he could see her on Ford's camera. They moved back and ducked around the corner. Josh came running toward them and ducked just in time. The bright light filled the screen as the explosion flashed, then light from where the door lead to the tunnel. Ford ran toward the doorway, Jax behind him and then Josh. Debris still floated in the air and obstructed his view now and then.

Gun shots fired and his eyes roamed the cameras to see where they came from. Suddenly he couldn't see any of his team, just what their cameras saw. Jax shot one of the men ducking behind a sofa, pointing a gun at her. Ford did the same. Soon Josh appeared on Jax's camera, as he hugged the wall but advanced further into the building. Ford followed behind but Jax stayed put. He saw her turn to check the entrance they just made then turn back to watch Ford and Josh.

Ford kicked open a door and flipped on the light then stepped back out. Josh did the same in another room. They continued on, and then Jax advanced toward them. Axel quietly reported, we're in.

He breathed a sigh of relief and watched as they advanced. Josh kicked in another door, looked inside then stepped out, and motioned to Jax. Must have found the office. She'd go in and look around while the rest of the team secured the rest of the house.

A motion on one of the cameras caught his attention, and he saw two men climbing out of an escape hatch in the mountain. Tapping the comm system he said, "Two men on the east side of the mountain just came out of an escape hatch about one hundred yards from the main entrance. Out."

Gaige's voice was low when he responded, "Copy. Wyatt?"

"On it."

More shots were fired within the house and his eyes darted to Jax in the office. She continued to rifle through drawers and files so she wasn't in the fray. Josh kicked a gun away then stepped over a dead body and he knew where the shots had come from. All Josh said was, "Three."

With the two that had run out and the three now dead inside, that meant five men in the Santarino compound working. Pulling up his phone he called Jared Timm, their computer guru extraordinaire. "Yeah."

"Jared, I need some information."

"Whatcha need brother?"

"Did either Victor or Mangus Santarino have kids? I don't recall any mention of any from either family."

Tapping could be heard on the other end of the line as his eyes watched the cameras. Wyatt had almost caught up with the two running down the mountain. They may be younger, but Wyatt was huge and those long strides of his made him run faster than you'd dream a man of his size could move.

"Yes, it seems Mangus and his wife, Sophia, have a daughter named Francesca."

"How is it that information was left out of all the reports we had?"

Tapping. Silence. More tapping. "Hmm, well it looks like after they had her, there was an attempt on Mangus' life and they sent her away. She went to the Italian countryside with caretakers and Sophia spent the majority of her time there with Francesca."

"There should have been hospital records."

"Nope, no hospital records. They've either been wiped or they never existed. The Santarinos are a very wealthy family so they probably paid someone to keep her birth off the record."

"How old is Francesca?"

"According to school records she's around twenty-four now."

"I don't know how you get this shit, Jared, but I'm damned glad you do."

"My bill is coming." Chuckling sounded then a click and the line went dead.

He checked Jax's camera and she was still looking through papers and tossing some into a briefcase she'd found alongside the desk so he allowed his eyes to float over to Wyatt. The two people Wyatt was closing in on both had short dark hair, jeans and button up white shirts. From this distance he couldn't tell if one of them was female, but he'd hear it as soon as Wyatt captured them.

Josh entered the office Jax was in and he could see her face on his camera. Her smile was breathtaking, even through all of this. He opened the comm unit to hear what she was saying. "I've found routes in and out of the country. I've got some of Mags's contacts in the Ozarks and I have shipping companies owned by the

Santarinos and the dummy companies to hide their ownership."

"Great work as usual, Jax."

She beamed at her brother again then continued to pack things up. Josh turned to look out the door then Ford announced, "All clear."

Wyatt's voice came over the comm units. "These are fucking girls."

*

Later, they convened at the compound to wrap up this mission. Gaige entered the conference room where they all waited for the final wrap up and release from this mission.

"Hey everyone, so I just got off the phone with my Federal contact. Mags is in jail, she's charged with a shit ton of federal crimes against her, so she won't see the light of day. Turns out, Georgia had a record in her country which is why she was so eager to come here and work for Mangus. It got her out of Dodge, so to speak." Nodding in his direction, Dodge smiled and nodded.

"They've rounded up the bodies and between you and me, my contact said he isn't happy about the body count, but it's less than last time, so he's counting that as a win. Plus, as a bonus they have the Santarino girl and her friend."

Chuckling around the table and a little ribbing between the team members halted Gaige's report, but he allowed it to happen. Bonding and all.

"Finally." Gaige's eyes met Jax's. "Jax, I'm sorry to have to tell you this, but Stan passed away this morning. Doctors said he didn't have long and turns out he didn't. He did tell a nurse at the hospital that you were the cutest little spitfire he'd ever met."

Jax's eyes watered and her shoulders slumped but she didn't break down and cry. Not yet anyway, but maybe later. She was a tough Little Mama. And he was in love with her.

"Okay, great job team. Hawk is being released today and I'm taking the Beast to pick him up. Bed rest for a few days, then therapy and he'll be good as new. Your pay will be deposited in the morning."

40

I'D NEVER MET YOU

L aughing, she threw her head back and enjoyed the way it felt to laugh. Megan and Skye sat across the table from her as Megan continued to tell the story she'd been entertaining them with for the past twenty minutes. They'd started doing girls' night, once a month about six months ago and she'd be lying if she said she didn't look forward to them. She'd never had girlfriends growing up. Their life was secretive given what her father did for a living. Plus she wasn't a Barbie and Ken girl. She liked shooting guns and wrestling boys to the ground to show them how strong she was. But, Megan needed friends because she was newer to the area and all alone up on that damned mountain. Except for Ford and Shelby, their daughter, but she needed girls to chat with about anything. Skye was from the area and because she and Skye were practically neighbors, it seemed natural for these women to join together and become friends. They shared so much. Their husbands, Megan and Skye's, worked in the same company as Dodge and Jax. She couldn't have secrets with them because they knew everything anyway.

But, as nice as it was to have girls' night out, and friends, she always found herself kind of missing Dodge while she was out. She'd grown to love him so damned much these past six months. It was mind boggling how much.

Skye tapped her forefinger on top of the back of Jax's hand, which lay on the table top. "Stop thinking about Dodge again. You're so damned lovesick you make us look bad."

Giggling she responded. "I'm not lovesick. And what makes you think I'm thinking about him?"

Megan laughed. "You're kidding, right? You get this far-off dreamy look in your eyes and you disappear into your head."

"Shut up."

"You shut up." Skye retorted. "Next time, I'll take your picture so you can see your lovesick face."

Both of her friends laughed and she joined in. Then a feeling fell over her, a feeling you get when you think someone is watching you. Slowly panning the Saturday night crowd at the Copper Cup, she looked over at the bar and there he sat. Watching her. He titled his glass in her direction and winked.

Standing she grabbed her glass and slowly walked toward the bar, keeping the handsome man in her sight. Three women hovered behind him, giggling and trying to get his attention, but she was thrilled to see his eyes stayed focused on hers.

Setting her glass on the top of the bar and standing at a 45-degree angle to him, she glanced over at the sexy man staring at her.

"Little Mama, you have no idea what you're getting into here."

She giggled. "You have no idea who I am or what I'm capable of, Tarzan."

He chuckled as he leaned in, his eyes bore into hers. "I think I do, Little Mama."

She inhaled deeply and the fresh scent of Dodge floated to her nostrils and she had to fight not to close her eyes and enjoy it. He interrupted her sensual thoughts, "As a matter of fact, I know what you're capable of so well, I know without a doubt that I want to experience it for the rest of my life. How about you, Little Mama? You want to spend your life with Tarzan? Ring, vows and all? Maybe a baby or two?"

Her eyes widened and her heart hammered in her chest so fast and furious she thought she'd pass out. Did he...? Holy crap! The sincere look in his eyes told her he meant it. Those green orbs so sexy and so very special to her. He reached across the corner of the bar and took her left hand in his left hand. With his right hand he pulled an incredible ring from his shirt pocket and slid it slowly onto her ring finger. The enormous pink diamond winked at her in it's simple setting then it began to swim and blur as tears sprang to her eyes.

"Really?"

He scoffed at her question but squeezed her hand, his thumb gently rubbing soothing strokes across the back of it. "I love you, Jax. I love you more than I ever dreamed I could love again. I love you more than I'll ever love anyone."

"Holy shit." Her voice cut off as her throat froze mid-sentence. He swiped at the tear that slid down her cheek and she saw him swallow hard; she realized that he was nervous about her answer. "Yes. Holy shit, yes."

Cheers went up behind her, but she didn't bother looking. Instead she jumped into his waiting arms and locked her lips onto his with an intensity she never had before. It didn't matter, he kissed her right back. When the crowd began to catcall she pulled away and once again looked him in the eyes. "I've never been proposed to before."

"I know. That's one of the things I love about you."

"That's stupid."

"No it's not. It's cool. You waited for me."

Someone grabbed her shoulders, spun her around, and then wrapped her into a big bear-hug. Her brother was here. Her brain didn't quite register what that meant. Then he said close to her ear. "Congratulations, Jacqueline. Mama's going to be so excited."

He passed her on to her female friends who were squealing with delight while grabbing at her hand to see the ring and congratulating her and Dodge. Then she saw their whole team standing around as they shook Dodge's hand, cheered them on, and bore witness to this momentous occasion.

After she'd been hugged by everyone she turned to Dodge, "You asked everyone to come here and watch?"

"No, I asked Josh for your hand in marriage and he told everyone that I was going to ask you. I hoped you'd say yes and then we'd need to celebrate, so I told them to stop by later. Apparently they all wanted to be here as witnesses. A few of them didn't think you'd say yes. You decide who that might be."

"Idiots." She laughed.

Looking down at her ring, the color of the diamond dawned on her and her heart swelled. "Is this...?"

"It is. It's part of the pink diamond you retrieved from Georgia. Guardwell's client allowed me to buy it from them with their blessing. I couldn't think of anything more appropriate."

"You know, Tarzan, you're pretty romantic."

"I never thought so, but then again, I'd never met you."

She kissed his lips softly and wrapped her arms around his waist, pulling him flush to her. The instant his arms wrapped around her, her heart sang. This was perfect and so much the life she never dreamed she'd have.

"And, I'd never met you."

Gaige stepped up to them and waved to the group to huddle. "Just got a call. We've got a new job and everyone needs to be at headquarters at 06:00.

Hawk chuckled and though he seldom said two words, he raised his glass as he toasted, "Here's to Dodge and Jax and a long happy life together."

   ***

Keep reading to meet Rory Richards and Alice Beggs from Rory: Finding His Match.

Rory: Finding His Match

Driving through the Eastern side of town, dog-ass tired and ready for bed, Rory glanced over at the gas station parking lot as he neared the intersection. Seeing what looked like a drug deal going down he quickly turned into the lot, directing his headlights at the two men exchanging a tiny bag for money.

Leaving his vehicle, Rory began walking toward the two men when they both took off running in different directions. Choosing to follow the man who'd taken the money he kept pace as best he could but he was losing ground as the spry and lanky drug dealer was scared and surely not interested in spending the night in jail.

He was likely a low-level dealer, but with enough pressure sometimes these guys gave up a higher up or two.

A gun shot rang out, then another. Diving behind a dumpster, which was some cover, but likely not enough, he glanced around the side in the direction of the shots. His heartbeat quickened, but luckily his senses seemed to increase as the adrenaline pumped through his body.

Seeing the flash of dark clothing duck behind the building before him, he crouched low and squat-walked to the side of the building, then slowly moved in the direction of his perp. His gun was out and pointed in the direction before him, his ears heard a slight crunching of feet on gravel. Slowly raising himself up, he pointed his gun toward the corner of the building and let up a quick prayer to be on-point today. No accidents.

A gun shot sounded and a bullet hit the building about a foot above his head. Quickly dropping to the ground he slowly let out a breath, inhaled once again and scrambled to the edge of the building where he'd thought his target had ducked behind.

Standing quickly and twisting his body to the side he moved around the building, the brick walls scratching his back as he hovered close.

Movement from the shadows and a flash of metal aimed at his head had him leveling his pistol back at this new target.

"DEA." She half whispered half yelled. Her voice was tight, her emotions likely as high as his.

"Lynyrd Station PD." He responded. Then wondered

where in the hell a DEA agent had come from. Lynyrd Station PD didn't have the luxury of a DEA agent.

They stood for a few seconds, each assessing the other, guns leveled on the other, emotions high.

She stepped into the sliver of light that shown from the overhead street lights and he damned near dropped his weapon. Familiar eyes stared back at him, the hypnotic green he'd remembered from years ago. Before he'd left the Army. Before he'd been married to Debra.

***

Get Rory: Finding His Match now to see what happens to these two as they battle emotions, criminals, and rules.

Get PJ's newsletter for updates on new releases, sales, fun snippets and so much more.

ENJOY THIS BOOK? YOU CAN MAKE A BIG DIFFERENCE.

Reviews are the most powerful tools in my arsenal when it comes to getting attention for my books. As much as I'd like to, I don't have the financial muscle of a New York publisher. I can't take out full page ads in the newspaper or put posters on the subway.

(Not yet, anyway.)

But I do have something much more powerful and effective than that, and it's something that those big publishers would die to get their hands on.

A committed and loyal bunch of readers.

Honest reviews of my books help bring them to the attention of other readers.

If you've enjoyed this book I would be so grateful to you if you could spend just five minutes leaving a review (it can be as short as you like) on the book's vendor page. You can jump right to the page of your choice by clicking below.

Thank you so very much.

ALSO BY PJ FIALA

Click here to see a list of all of my books with the blurbs.

Contemporary Romance

Rolling Thunder Series

Moving to Love, Book 1

Moving to Hope, Book 2

Moving to Forever, Book 3

Moving to Desire, Book 4

Moving to You, Book 5

Moving Home, Book 6

Moving On, Book 7

Second Chances Series

Designing Samantha's Love, Book 1

Securing Kiera's Love, Book 2

Military Romantic Suspense

Bluegrass Security Series

Heart Thief, Book One

· Finish Line, Book Two

Lethal Love, Book Three

Big 3 Security

Ford: Finding His Fire Book One

Lincoln: Finding His Mark Book Two

Dodge: Finding His Jewel Book Three

Rory: Finding His Match Book Four

GHOST

Defending Keirnan, GHOST Book One

Defending Sophie, GHOST Book Two

Defending Roxanne, GHOST Book Three

Defending Yvette, GHOST Book Four

Defending Bridget, GHOST Book Five

Defending Isabella, GHOST Book Six

RAPTOR

Saving Shelby, RAPTOR Book One

MEET PJ

.

PJ is the author of the exciting Rolling Thunder series, Bounty Hunters, Second Chances and Chandler County series. Soon, her GHOST series will be exciting readers with page turning military alphas and the women who love them.

Her online home is https://www.pjfiala.com. You can connect with PM on Facebook at https://www.facebook.com/PJFialaı, on Twitter at @pfiala and Instagram at https://www.Instagram.com/PJFiala. If you prefer to email, go ahead, she'll respond - pjfiala@pjfiala.com.